Where the Atlantic Meets the Land

Where the Atlantic meets the Land

BY CALDWELL LIPSETT

BOSTON: ROBERTS BROS., 1896
LONDON: JOHN LANE, VIGO ST.

gift

W

2.

L 7.

Lipsett

Where the Atlantic
Meets the Land

CALDWELL, CLIFF

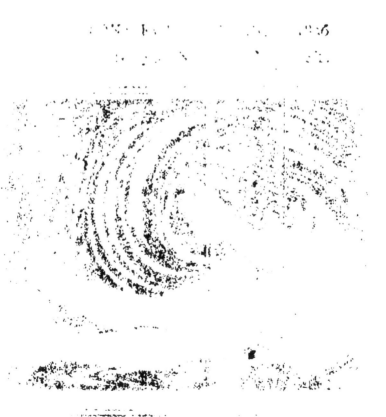

Where the Atlantic meets the Land

BY CALDWELL LIPSETT

BOSTON: ROBERTS BROS., 1896
LONDON: JOHN LANE, VIGO ST.

𝔘𝔫𝔦𝔳𝔢𝔯𝔰𝔦𝔱𝔶 𝔓𝔯𝔢𝔰𝔰:

JOHN WILSON AND SON, CAMBRIDGE, U. S. A.

DEDICATED

TO

MY DEAREST MOTHER.

CONTENTS

CONTENTS

THE UNFORGIVEN SIN

BELLA SWEENY and Terry Gallagher had a holiday, and were spending it upon the rocks at Kilcross. He was a groom and she was a maid at 'the big house,' some miles inland, and this was her first visit to the place. He had been there several times before, and was doing the honors of the scenery. They had been 'coortin' for some time, and he sat with his arm round her waist, in silence for the most part, punctuated by occasional references to the local names for heads of the landscape: he kept severely to facts, with the practical mind of the peasant class from which he sprang.

The point at which they found themselves was the innermost end of the long line of black-faced cliffs, where the rocky strata suddenly ceased and gave way to the sandy lowlands. The rock upon which they were seated was a single flat slab, which extended a hundred

I

yards into the sea, forming a natural break-
water for the little cove behind them. To their
right there stretched inland a couple of miles of
yellow glistening strand, which merged gradually in the tufted bent-grass and rounded
hillocks of the dunes which sloped to meet it
at high-water mark. At the furthest point of
sight in this direction, the rocky strata cropped
up again in the shape of an immense reef which
stretched out half a mile into the sea, and now
at low tide lay like a gigantic alligator on the
surface of the water. When the tide was full
its jagged points were completely covered, and
only a thread of surf was left to warn the fisherman of its hidden dangers.

'This rock that we're a-settin' on,' said Terry,
'is called the Yeough Flag, from the fishes they
catch off ov it: an' yon big wan out there is
Carrick Fad: an' that wan is the Connaught-
man's Rock, where a boat's load from Connaught
was wrecked wan winter's night an' all han's
lost.' He pointed as he spoke to a spot in the
sea beside them, where a mat of long golden
brown wrack floated flush with the surface, and
the swell broke gently with a soft gurgle and a
few air-bubbles.

Behind them and to their left the cliffs rose
two hundred feet in the air as they soared
seaward. The first fifty feet were formed of
crumbling slate, above that came a layer of
gravelly soil which was scooped out in regular
scollops by land slips and seamed and scarred
by winter torrents. At the extreme point of
the bay the rock was hollowed out beneath by
the constant dash of the surf, and the bank
sloping more gently overhead was clothed with
the long rank grass which has never known a
scythe, coarse like the hairs of a horse's tail.
The diamond-shaped point where the two met
cut sharply into the sky-line. Beyond that point
the cliffs became one solid wall of beetling rock.

The space between the base of the cliffs and
the edge of the water in the cove was covered
with boulders piled pell-mell on top of each
other: they were of every size, from a trunk
to a small house, and of every shape: here a
square-shaped block lay like a stranded whale
and there a thin slab was tilted edgeways
towards the sky. The *débris* of the Atlantic
flung by winter storms here upon its outermost
verge, looking like the deposit of some huge
primeval glacier.

'Yon 's the Cormorants' Rock,' interjected Terry, alluding to the pointed headland, 'an' there 's a cormorant,' as he pointed to a black speck winging its way with steady flight low down across the water.

Then he continued with a sudden change of subject, blurting out the words as though they blistered his tongue, 'Bella, darlin', don't you think we 've waited long enough?...I 've got enough to marry on now. When shall we be called?' He had been nerving himself for this effort all the morning, and gave a great sigh of relief now that it was over.

The girl sat silent for a minute, considering the question thoughtfully, and then replied quite calmly, 'Av ye 're of the wan min' this day six months, come an' tell me, an' I 'll let you give notice to the praste,' and she lifted her mouth for the official stamp to the agreement.

For some time after that they sat in awkward silence. Both of them tried to think of a remark, but neither could find one. The growing uneasiness of an anti-climax rose between them. His arm relaxed round her waist, he shuffled his feet restlessly, and at last jumping up, exclaimed:

'Let 's go an' catch some s'rimps.'

'What 's that?' asked Bella.

'Little wee fishes that sweem about in the pools over there.'

'D'ye think ye can catch them?' she inquired doubtfully, but she rose and accompanied him to the rock-strewn side of the cove opposite, which proved on closer view to be dotted with small pools left by the retreating tide. In these a small variety of prawns disported themselves, and were dislodged from behind stones and underneath pieces of seaweed by Terry's intrusive ash-plant. He knelt down and tried to catch some of them in his hands, but they retreated warily in front of him with outstretched feelers; and when apparently enclosed upon all sides, darted with a sudden spring out of reach, and retired backwards under the impenetrable fastness of an overhanging rock.

'These yellah wans is rock s'rimps,' he explained, 'sand s'rimps is gray.'

Bella was greatly delighted with the queer aspect of the creatures, their translucent bodies, the large heads with their serrated horn and protruding eyes, and the long flexible 'whiskers,' and begged her lover to catch one for her to see closer.

Presently they came to a large pool above the reach of any but the highest tides. The water here softened by the rain was only brackish: the stones were clothed with long green seaweed, and those underneath the stagnant surface were coated with a brownish slime. The shrimps imprisoned by a chance migration in this uncongenial spot were more sluggish than their tidal neighbors, and one allowed himself to be caught, and in a moment lay kicking on Bella's outstretched palm.

When she had looked her fill of admiration Terry put it for greater safekeeping in his mouth: at this indignity the shrimp mustered all its activity for a final effort and jumped, tail first, down the young man's throat. Terry commenced to cough and splutter and went purple in the face, and Bella in alarm hit him a violent slap between the shoulders.

Her action had the desired effect, for it dislodged the shrimp from its dangerous restingplace, but a blow from her vigorous young arm was no light matter, and Terry lurched forward onto a tuft of the green seaweed which slid away beneath his feet: to recover his balance he stepped hastily onto a brown stone in the centre of the pool, but it proved yet more treacherous than the green: his heels flew from beneath him, leaving long nail marks on the greasy surface of the stone, and he fell flat on his back in the shallow water.

He lay still for a moment, stunned by the surprise, then rose to his feet, his clothes dripping streams of water and his hair matted with the long green seaweed, and found Bella shaking with a great spasm of laughter. Her large serious gray eyes were completely closed, and her pretty face contorted with the vulgarity of excessive merriment. He grinned sheepishly and said, —

' Them stones is powerful slippy.'

But she only laughed the more, till she became so weak that she collapsed onto the nearest rock, the tears streaming down her cheeks. At the sight a vague resentment gradually crept over Terry's docile Irish nature: he felt dimly that no woman would laugh like that at a man whom she really loved, and the change worked in the appearance of her features annoyed him. He exclaimed sharply, —

' Ah, quit now. Much you care av I 'd been choked.'

Bella looked up, surprised at the unusual tone, but stopped laughing at once and replied meekly:

' Niver heed me, Terry, dear, I did n't offer to vex yous.'

Peace was at once restored, and they began to scramble together hand in hand over the uneven rocks towards the sea. All that was now left of it in the bay was a single streak of silver, which lay pent and sleeping in its narrow channel, that had been worn deep in the solid rock by the current of ages. Its bottom was piled with serpentine coils of wrack, sea-ferns in all their varied beauty of form and color, and ' slock-morrows ' with their thick hairy stems and long slimy leaves: some of them still gripped with their roots the stones which they had torn with them beneath the stress of storm from their ocean bed. Beneath the misty film of the breeze upon the surface the whole mass writhed with each recurring pulse of the unresting sea like a living welter of sea-snakes.

' That 's the wrack-hole,' announced Terry the well informed.

' Let me see,' said Bella, clinging timidly to his arm as she crept nearer and peered into its depths, with a shrinking awe as though at some half-human monster that battened upon mankind. For its name was known through the countryside as the bane of widows and childless mothers: at half-tide the waves poured over the surrounding rocks and swept seaward through this passage in a race that the strongest swimmer could not stem, and which had hurried many a venturesome beginner to his doom.

But many a time in the after days Terry looked back upon that moment, when the girl beside him clung to his hand and confided in his protection, as the happiest in his life. Such trifles serve to uplift or cast down a lover.

Bella shuddered and drew back, and they passed onwards towards the Cormorants' Rock. The boulders ceased and they came out upon the flat bed-rock. Women were there gathering sloak and dillusk, the spinach and edible moss of the sea: the constant passage of generations of naked feet had worn a track smooth and free from barnacles over the flaky slate: a row of footholds carved by the same agency led round the projecting corner, which was whitened down to high-water mark by the droppings of the cormorants from their nightly roosting-places above.   As they looked, a couple of the women attempted the passage.   The day was calm, but the Atlantic is never still, and rising out of nothing 'the shining sensitive silver of the sea ' broke with a dull murmur upon this outpost of the cliff.   The women waited until a wave larger than usual had passed, and began their journey, but the treacherous sea regathered itself and was upon them in the midst, dashing up beneath their petticoats. They flattened their bodies desperately against the rock, and twined their fingers in the short button-wrack that grew at high-water mark: their skirts floated wide upon the surface of the swell, but its force did not avail to pluck them from their hold.   It retreated baffled, and the two bedraggled figures scrambled round the corner and were lost to view.

' Holy Mother, but it 's a mercy they were n't lost,' cried Bella.

' Ay,' replied Terry, ' the tide must have turned.   It 's top spring the day, so it must be afther twelve.   Troth, it 's near hand wan,' he continued, cocking his eye at the sun.   It was n't often that he had the opportunity to unload such a store of information, and he made the best of the occasion.

Bella regarded him with wide eyes as he displayed this unsuspected hoard of marine lore, and treated him with unwonted respect for the remainder of the day.

' It 's time we was goin' home, or I 'll be late for the milkin',' she said, and they began to retrace their steps.

When they got off the boulders once more onto the sandy floor of the little bay, the tide was coming in with long pauses and feigned retreats followed by sudden rushes. In the midst of its path stood an isolated altar of four large stones just islanded by a tongue of bubbling wavelets.

' I mind when I was a wee fellah,' said Terry, ' we used to see which of us could stay on them foor stones longest without gettin' wet.'

' Let 's try,' cried Bella, gleefully.

They jumped onto the stones and off again in eager rivalry for several minutes. Often there would be a wide gulf between them and the shore, and then the sea would retreat and leave 'it bare again. But at last they stopped too long: the tide flowed in with a sudden rush and never came back again near their island.

'What will we do?' cried Bella in dismay, when she realized they were altogether surrounded.

'Niver fear,' replied Terry, 'I can carry yous,' and he took off his shoes and stockings well pleased at the success of his stratagem.

He took her up carefully in his arms, like a baby, and carried her ashore: she lay quite still, without a blush or tremor, as he strained her to his breast, and when he kissed her before setting her upon her feet her lips met his frankly but did not return their pressure. Terry knew little of the ways of women, but his instinct told him that either more or less warmth would have been a better augury. He felt 'a bit dashed,' as he himself would say, at her tolerant attitude.

Then he went and put the horse into the cart, which he had borrowed for the day from a neighbor. Bella sat in the bottom upon a lining of hay, and her teeth rattled in her head at every jolt of the springless vehicle behind the rough-trotting plough-horse. Terry sat on the shaft in front, swinging his legs, and got a crick in his neck turning his head to admire her dishevelled hair and the brown shadows beneath her Irish eyes, ' rubbed in with a dirty finger,' as the saying goes.

For the next six months Terry lived upon the memory of that day. It formed the high-water mark of his influence with the girl whom he grew to love the more she disregarded him: for a man's love feeds upon starvation. Upon that day the unfamiliarity of her surroundings had allowed him to appear to an advantage he had never enjoyed before or since. Up to that point in their intercourse she had always been the stronger, and now a new element appeared to have entered her life and ousted him from it. Nothing that he could say or do could touch her interest any longer: he had an impalpable feeling that every day he was more outside of her, more in the cold. When they met about their daily work upon the farm, she merely tolerated his presence as she would tolerate a necessary article of furniture.

Terry racked his brains vainly to guess what cause of offence he had given her, or to imagine a reason for this change in her attitude: but he could find none. It was true that of late ' the misthress' had taken Bella to wait upon herself exclusively with the exception of her work in the dairy: and some of the other maids threw out hints about 'them as is took notice of soon becomes overly cocked up:' but Terry knew her too well to suspect her of such little-ness: he rather put down her evident weariness of him to some failure in himself, he was not good enough for her.

One day in especial this came home to him. She had driven into the neighboring town of Lisnamore with her mistress, Mrs. Fenwick, to accompany that lady upon a shopping excursion. He was passing down the opposite side of the street, and saw her sitting upon the side of the car talking with a heightened color to 'the young Masther,' Mrs. Fenwick's eldest son, who was home from Trinity for the vacation, and who was standing with one hand resting carelessly upon the cushion beside her. She did not even notice Terry, and he passed on with a desolate feeling at his heart, nearer to tears than he had been since his babyhood.

On the afternoon that the six months expired he went to find her in the byre at milking time. He had questioned himself long and anxiously if it was worth while going at all, but came to the conclusion 'best give her her chanst.' So though he had already seen her several times that day, he went to his room over the coach-house and put on his Sunday clothes, the clothes he had worn that day upon the rocks at Kilcross, and a flaming scarlet tie that he had bought for this occasion a week afterwards. And in this gala dress with his heart in his boots he went to meet his fate.

He stood with a straw in his mouth leaning against the doorpost of the byre, and never said a word from the moment when the first thin thread of milk spirted into the empty tin porringer with a tinkling sound till the last porringer was emptied into the foaming pails. He walked beside her in solemn silence while she carried the pails to the dairy: but though his heart yearned over her he did not offer to help her: the men of the country do not relieve the women of their burdens. And still in silence he watched her pour the fresh milk through the strainer into the large earthenware crocks to ' set ' for cream.

At last Bella herself broke the silence. ' Well, Terry, are ye ov the wan min' yet?' she asked abruptly in a mocking voice.

' I am,' replied Terry heavily, ' av ye'll take me.'

Bella flushed and looked down, then she continued suddenly in a hard, even tone:

'I'll not marry yous here.   But av ye like to come wid me to Enniskilling, I'll marry yous to-morrow.'

At this unlooked for speech the blood surged over Terry's face and neck in a deep red flood.   'Ov coorse I'll come and welcome,' he answered hastily: the opportunity was too good to miss, there would be time to think later on.

But the moment that she had obtained her terms thus easily a swift remorse seized upon the girl, and she cried:

'No, no, I won't go.   It's not fair on yous.   I don't luv yous enough.'

But the young man replied firmly with a deep note of exaltation in his voice:

'I have yer promus, and I won't give it yous back.   I know that I haven't yer luv yet, but I'm not afeard but I can win it, av ye give me the chanst.   I'd come av I had to wade through a fiel' ov fire.'

Suddenly the girl burst into a flood of tears, and bowing her head, seized his hand and kissed it, murmuring through her sobs,

'You are too good for me, Terry, too good for me.'

'Too good,' he repeated wonderingly, resting his hand uncouthly upon her bright brown hair. 'Is it me? Why, I'm not fit for yous to wipe yer little feet upon.'

The next evening at the twilight hour there was a small gathering at the forge, which was perched upon the side of a hill upon the main road near the centre of the parish: it stood a little back in a square open space with its staring whitewashed walls, thatched roofs, and large unglazed window-openings. It was the district club, the meeting-place for the scattered cottagers of the countryside, the centre whence gossip radiated. The blacksmith was just finishing the last of a set of horseshoes, and the roar of the bellows formed a monotonous undertone to the fitful conversation. Patsey Brannigan, the patriarch of the place, was sitting on his usual creel, with his short clay pipe between his teeth, watching the sparks fly from the glowing metal with unblinking eyes. A group of half a dozen young men lounged about the doorway, propping the doorposts upon either side. Mac Ilrea dropped the completed shoe into the trough of water with a spluttering hiss, and said in a tone of relief, ' There, that 's done, glory be.'

At that moment Hannah Sweeny, Bella's cousin, came up, carrying a couple of pails of water from the well, and put them down in front of the doorway as she asked the company at large:

' Have ye heard tell what our Bella's afther doin'?'

' De'il a hate', said Owen Gallagher, ' shpake away.'

' She 's aff to Enniskilling with Terry Gallagher:' she was a red-headed girl with bare feet, and she stood with her hands on her hips as she watched the effect of her announcement.

' What, that gomeral,' exclaimed Owen in disgust. He was a connection of Terry's in a place where there are whole groups of families of the same name, and the blood is inextricably mingled; but the relationship was only close enough to throw into relief the uneasy rivalry with which he regarded his cousin.

' Yis, they wint be the mornin' thrain. An' what's more,' she continued, doling out her news with the deliberation that comes of a

momentary importance, ' they do be sayin' that
oul' Peggy's gone afther them be the evenin'
thrain.'

' That's as it shud be,' said Mrs. Mac, coming
forward from the inner room, ' her mother has a
right to see they 're married proper.'

' What she cud see in yon suckin' calf, bets
ahl,' continued Owen, harping upon his one
note.

' Troth thin it 's him that might do betther
than thrapesin' about the counthry afther yon
flibbertigibbet,' said Hannah with heat.

'Ay,' replied her antagonist with a leer, 'yous
had ahlways a saft spot for him yersilf, I doubt,'
and the girl retired defeated from the contest.

' What bets me,' said Mac slowly, ' is what ud
ail them not to be married quiet at home.
Who 's hinderin' them ? '

A s'gh passed through the group as they
settled themselves down to consider this new
aspect of the case.

Suddenly old Patsey took the pipe out of his
mouth and spat upon the ground, then he leant
forward deliberately while every one waited, took
a red-hot turf coal from the fire with his naked
fingers and sucked at it with his dhudeen,

gradually cramming it down into the bowl until it had all crumbled away, then he said:

'Andy Sweeny's dahter cud n't do other.'

'Ah,' said one of the younger men interrogatively.

'He was a wild shpark, he was,' continued Patsey, meditatively, 'I doubt it 's the father's blood she has in her. He was terrible fond of the gurls, so he was,' and the old man shook his head over a failing that had never appealed to him, and did not belong to his race.

'What call had oul' Peggy to take the likes ov yon?' asked Mac.

'Ahl ov us is young wanst in our lives,', replied Patsey sententiously, 'and he was a terrible han'some man. He was not from these parts, a packman from down Longford way: an' Masther Johnnie, what 's home from school —'

'College,' corrected Hannah, but nobody paid any heed to her.

'— he has a power ov book-larnin', and he did be sayin' to me the other day that Sweeny come ov Spanish blood that they have in them down yonder from the times the Armady was wrecked on the shores of Longford —'

'Sorra but Longford is n't near the say,' interrupted Hannah, ' troth I larnt that meself in the National School — '

' Ah, will ye hould yer whisht, Hannah Gallagher, ye long-tongued divil ye,' cried Mrs. Mac. 'Ye 're too cliver be half wid yer jography, so yous are.'

Hannah subsided, and Patsey continued, serenely impervious to criticism.

' Anyways she married him, and she only regretted it wanst, and that was ivery day ov her life afther. He was killed in a fight at a fair over a gurl, and that was the ind ov him, pace to his ashes.'

' Ye wud n't think oul' Peggy was that soort now,' persisted Mac; ' she lukes as could as yon hearthstone,' pointing as he spoke to the heap of gray ashes that had lately been a fire.

But one of the young men leant upon the handle of the bellows, and in a moment they leapt into a fierce white flame.

' Ay,' said Patsey, pointing the stem of his clay at the quickly-blackening cinders, ' yon 's a betther answer nor any I cud give in a month ov Sundays.'

The following morning the rumor ran through the whole townland like fire through flax that Bella had returned with her mother unaccompanied by Terry, and unmarried.

Many were the conjectures that evening at the forge as to the meaning of this new move. Terry had been sounded on the subject, and told all he knew.   He went with Bella to Enniskillen, and gave notice to the priest.   Then they were overtaken by old Peggy, who spoke to her daughter privately for a few minutes. Bella came out from the conversation and said she had changed her mind and would not marry him after all.   He raved and stormed, but all to no purpose: Bella was indifferent and her mother sphinx-like, he could get nothing further out of either, and he could not marry the girl in spite of herself.   She went away and slept with her mother that night, and returned home by the first train in the morning.   He could no nothing but follow her by the second. — Those were the facts, but as to the explanation of them he was entirely at a loss.

While they were still discussing this strange story, Terry himself passed the forge, switching moodily with his ash-plant at the ' boughaleen bwees,' the yellow rag-weed, that fringed the roadside.

When he came opposite the group at the doorway his cousin Owen called out to him jeeringly, ' Well, Terry, so yous are home again wid wan han' as long as the other. Did n't oul' Peggy think yous good enough for her dahter? '

Terry halted and looked up at them with a mild, wistful expression in his oxlike eyes, the look of a wounded animal, and said simply, ' Shure I 'm not good enough for her.'

Somehow the laugh that had begun died away immediately, and Owen withdrew behind his companions, and began to light his pipe in a dark corner of the forge. His pipe was already alight. But Terry went upon his way pondering these, the first rough words of outside criticism that had fallen upon his ears. His mind was slow to move, and needed a jog from another hand to start it : but once stirred it moved deeply, and entertaining few ideas it was all the more tenacious of those which did manage to effect an entrance. His fancy for Bella, at first a young man's liking for a maid, had been fanned by opposition till now it had become a slow fire consuming his marrow. He thought of her all day, and in the night he lay awake biting his pillows, to prevent himself crying aloud for very loneliness of spirit. Bella remained at home with her mother, and he never saw her now, but her picture was too indelibly printed on his imagination for propinquity to add to her charms: absence but idealized them. He went about his work brooding eternally over his loss, and for the first time no one ventured to intrude upon his solitude. They laughed at him behind his back for a soft who had been jilted at the altar: but he had acquired a fresh dignity, which saved him from open ridicule or unsolicited advances. In those days when his trouble lay heavy upon him he shunned human creatures and found companionship only in the society of his horses. Their large calm soothed his fevered nerves. They grew to know his step, and whinnied when they heard him coming: and they would caress him with their tender muzzles as he rubbed them down with the soft hissing noise that they loved. For in sorrow animals are our most comforting companions: they are so silent and placid and self-contained, ' not one is respectable or unhappy over the whole earth.'

But at the end of six months a fresh shock

convulsed the neighborhood. As on the first occasion it was Hannah that brought the news to the forge, but this time it was the morning, and there was nobody there but the blacksmith and his wife.

'Have ye heerd tell what's come to oul' Peggy's Bella,' she asked, standing breathlessly in the doorway, and added without waiting for a reply, 'she had a child last night.'

'You don't tell me,' cried Mrs. Mac in amazement.

'They had the oul' wumman from the Poor-house there ahl night, an' I just seen the dishpensary docther lave the dure this minute wid me own two eyes.'

'An' her such a soft-spoken crathur,' continued Mrs. Mac; 'ye'd think that butther wud n't melt in her mouth, but it's ahlways them soort that goes wrong.'

Swiftly the news spread, and by half-past twelve at dinner-time all the workers in the fields about had left their haymaking, for it was harvest-time once more, to gather at this central spot and discuss the situation.

At first everybody was incredulous: such an event was almost unheard of in a community where chastity was a tradition, and insufficient nutriment kept the blood thin and the passions cold. But soon the testimony of a neighbor who had been called in put the question of fact beyond doubt.

'What did I tell ye about Andy Sweeny's dahter?' said old Patsey, taking credit for his half-prophecy in the fuller light of after events.

'Ay, ay, deed so,' murmured the group in chorus.

Then curiosity centred itself on the point of who was the father of the child.

'It cudn't be Terry Gallagher, now,' said Mrs. Mac judicially, 'troth I'll be boun' he knew nahthin' about it, the crathur.'

'Ah, him is it?' said Owen contemptuously, 'he's too great a fule.'

'He's had a lucky escape anyways,' continued Mrs. Mac meditatively, 'I wunner now why she didn't marry him when she had the chanst, an' no wan wud ha' been a hate the wiser. Oul' Peggy 'll be quare an' mad that she stopped the weddin'.'

'I cud make a boul' guess then,' broke in Hannah, who had been waiting for an opening. 'I'll houl' ye I know who owns it, an' more

shame for her to lave her own wans for them
as does n't want her now that she 's in trouble.
I 'm thinkin' it 's some of the quality has a
finger in it.'

' Betther kape a still tongue in yer head about
the quality,' interrupted the blacksmith hastily,
' laste said 's soonest mended.'

' Here 's himself,' interjected one of the group
by the door warningly, as Terry came into sight,
climbing the hill towards them. As he drew
near it could be seen that his steps were hurried
and uneven, and his face as white as chalk.

He came straight up to them, and asked in
a tense whisper, ' Is it thrue?' looking from
one to the other.

They all avoided his eye and looked uneasily
away, except Owen, in whose breast the memory
of his self-humiliation of six months ago still
rankled. He stepped a pace forward, and
answered, —

' Aye, it sames you was good enough for her
afther ahl.'

His cousin looked at him with a lack-lustre
eye, as though he did not take in the meaning
of the words, and, encouraged by his quiescence,
Owen continued in a more pronounced tone, —

'More like it was her that was n't good
enough for yous.'

For a moment Terry stood rooted to the
spot, while the blood surged upwards and
veiled his eyesight with a mist, then he crouched
and sprang headlong at his adversary's throat
with an inarticulate snarl like a wild beast.

Owen was borne backwards by the impetus
of his weight, and fell striking his head against
the spike of the anvil: and Terry was torn
from him by two of the men, his eyes staring
and his limbs trembling with rage. When they
released their hold of him, his sinews, all un-
strung by the violence of his passion, gave way
beneath him and he collapsed in a heap upon
the floor. For a moment he sat there: then he
rose to his knees, and thence to his feet, and
staggered out of the door and down the road,
reeling to and fro in the sunlight like a drunken
man.

'Who 'd ha' thought it?' said Patsey, looking
after him: 'It 's wunnerful what stuff a taste of
the gurls does be makin' into a man. Yon wan
was a suckin' calf a while ago, and now he 's a
young bull.'

'May the divil roast him,' exclaimed Owen,

scrambling to his feet, and looking regretfully
at the pool of his own blood upon the floor.
' He has me disthroyed, but I 'll be even wid
him yit.'

When his momentary rage had died down a
great tumult was left in Terry's mind. The
scene which he had just passed through had
brought sharply home to him the attitude that
the neighbors would take towards Bella's trans-
gression. He pictured her to himself defenceless
before her persecutors, and longed to give her
the shelter of his arm and of his name. But
could he offer to marry her still, and consent to
be pointed at for the remainder of his life as
the husband of a wanton? for scandal dies hard
in the country. On the one side was ranged
the whole force of a public opinion which it
had never entered into his head to question
until now, and of his own inherited racial instincts, and on the other his great love for this
girl. He could not put it into words, but he
felt dimly within him that it was she herself
that he loved, and that her outward actions did
not affect her inward essence, that he knew her
better than any neighbor, and was a better
judge of her than blind convention. He was

not strong enough yet to be himself in the face
of his world, but the balance wavered ever
more deeply on the side of this new self that he
was discovering.   That he should have an
opinion of his own at all was a great advance
upon anything that he could have felt a year
ago.   But there is no forcing-house for the
growth of character like disappointed love.

At the end of a fortnight he was still wavering
in mind, but he could no longer rest without
seeing Bella.   So he put on his holiday suit, and
went down the road towards her mother's cottage; but this time he did not wear the scarlet
tie.   As he approached the house he realized that
it had a forlorn and neglected air, as though it
shared the fallen estimation of its occupants;
the grass grew thickly in the front yard and
upon the thatched roof, and the geraniums upon
the window-sill were withered and unwatered.

He pushed open the half-door and entered
unasked, as was his wont.   Bella was seated in
the window, working at her sprigging and
rocking a small wooden cradle with her foot;
at the sound of his footstep she looked up with
a strained hungry light in her eye, but at the
sight of him a shade of disappointment flitted

across her face and she continued to look past him over his shoulder as though expecting some one else. The old woman was seated on a three-legged stool crouched over the hearth while she stirred an iron pot of stirabout with a wooden pot-stick; she did not even turn her head when he entered.

' God save all here,' said Terry, awkwardly standing in the middle of the floor. His head nearly touched the blackened beam which ran across the middle of the room and supported a half-floor, whence the mingled smell of apples and dried onions came distinctly to his nostrils. He coughed and sat down upon the edge of the nearest chair, tucking his feet well under the rail and crunching his soft felt hat nervously in his hands. The swish of the thread being drawn through the embroidery was the only sound that broke the stillness, as he watched the regular sweep of Bella's arm against the window-pane.

' What 's yer wull, Terry Gallagher?' snapped old Peggy abruptly, after a time.

Terry turned his hat over several times, examined the lining very carefully, and finally replied to her question with another:

' Why did n't ye let on to me yon time, mother, and let me marry her while there was time ? '

At this heathenish question old Peggy rose to her full height and pointed the pot-stick accusingly at her daughter, as she said in a tone of concentrated bitterness :

' I wud n't let a wumman like yon soil an honest man's hearth. '

Bella sat unmoved, without taking the slightest notice of the words. Her mother and Terry belonged to a world outside of her which no longer affected her by their phantom movements.

But at this embodiment of the ghostly voices which he had been fighting against so long Terry sprang to his feet. In the face of concrete opposition a blind antagonism seized him which swallowed up all hesitation, and he dared to be individual. He took a stride forward, and, throwing out one arm towards the girl, said in a loud voice as though to penetrate her understanding :

' Bella, darlin', I 'll marry ye now, av ye 'll have me. '

Bella looked up with a faint smile of surprise, and opened her lips to answer. At that moment a thin cry came from the cradle at her feet; at the sound, while she still looked at him, a light crept over her face which transfigured it.

Then Terry knew that he had seen for the first time the love-look on a woman's face, and it was not for him.   And, boor as he was, the knowledge came home to him at that instant, that for any one to marry her save the man who had the power to raise that look upon her face would be a sacrilege.

He turned with drooped head, and stumbled out of the cabin without a word.

THE LEGEND OF BARNES-MORE GAP

AT the point where the range of mountains which divides the Northern from the Southern half of Donegal approaches nearest to the innermost extremity of Donegal Bay, there is a wild and rocky pass which, from a distance, shows as a saddle-shaped hollow on the sky-line, giving the impression of a bite taken by the mouth of a giant clean out of the centre of the mountain.

This gorge is still, as it always has been in the past, the main artery of communication between the level and fertile plains of Tyrone and Londonderry and the tract of country south of the mountains extending as far as Lough Erne. It is called Barnesmore Gap, and the following is the legend current upon the countryside as to the origin of the name.

' I tell the tale as 't was told to me.'

At the beginning of this century when Mr. Balfour's light railways were not thought of, and even the Finn Valley Railway as yet was not, its place was taken in the internal economy of the country by the highroad running through the Gap. Great then was the congestion of traffic and the indignation of traders far and wide, when a highwayman selected the part of this road which lay amidst the mountains for the scene of his depredations, and levied toll upon all comers.

Men of a peace-loving disposition or with time to spare diverted their course round the southern extremity of the range. And as time is the least valuable commodity in Ireland and usually the least considered, the general stream of commerce followed this direction. But there were cases where urgency or impatience led to the use of the old route, and off these the highwayman made his profit.

When this state of siege had continued for some time, a gentleman of Enniskillen of the name of O'Connor had need of a sum of two hundred pounds within a certain time. This money he had to get from Derry. But he could not trust the mail, which was regularly robbed, and it would not reach him in time by any route but the shortest — that through the Gap. None of his servants would run the risk of a meeting with the highwayman, and he had determined to take the journey himself, when a half-witted hanger-on about the house, named Blazing Barney from the color of his hair, volunteered for the service.

This man was a natural or a ' bit daft,' as they call it in Scotland. But his master knew that he could be sharp enough upon occasion, and no one would dream that such a half-witted creature would be trusted with such an important commission. Altogether this was the best chance of deceiving the highwayman, so he decided to risk it.

He offered Barney the pick of his weapons and his best hunter, but the omadhawn preferred to go unarmed and mounted upon the worst looking horse in the stable, an old gray, that was blind of one eye and lame of one leg, but could still do a good day's travelling. As he shrewdly remarked:

' Fwhat 'ud I be doin' on a gran' upstandin' baste like yon; the thafe beyant wud rise till the thrick in no time.'

For Barney's silliness only came on in fits at
the season of the new moon; at other times he
was merely a slightly exaggerated type of that
mixture of simplicity with a certain low-bred
cunning in practical matters which has dis-
tinguished the countryman in all ages from the
larger-minded dweller in cities. The present
was a lucid interval, so he could be trusted to
take care of himself.

So Barney jogged along on his way towards
Derry, through Fermanagh and Donegal, without fear of any ill, and only had to ask for
what he wanted in the way of food and shelter
in order to get it. The simple-hearted peasantry
never grudge ' bit nor sup ' to the poor of their
own order, and those afflicted as he was they
regard as being under the special protection of
heaven.

With the help of an early start, in spite of
the sorriness of his nag, he managed the fifty
miles between Enniskillen and the town of
Donegal on the first day, and early on the
second reached the Gap. It was a moist,
drizzling morning, and as he rode in among
the mountains a damp mist closed down upon
him, almost hiding the ground beneath him

from his sight.   The road passed upwards along the mountain side, until it became a mere ledge jutting out from it, and forming a break in the sheer descent of the cliff; on the one hand was a precipice, from the bottom of which came the ripple of rushing waters to warn the traveller from its brink, on the other rose the steep hillside, whence he could hear above him the muffled crowing of the grouse among the heather.

Suddenly a gigantic figure outlined itself upon the mist, seeming to Barney larger than human, and he crossed himself as he rode nearer to it.   But as the deceitful folds of vapor rolled away from it, the figure resolved itself into a man on horseback standing across the roadway at its narrowest point.

'Where are ye for?' said the stranger shortly.

'It's a saft day, yer 'ahner, an' where am I for, is it? Well, I'll just tell ye, it's Derry I'm for, that same, an' mebbe ye'll infarm me if I'm on the right road.' And Barney giggled vacantly.

'What are you laughing at, fool?'

'Laffin' is it me, yer 'ahner? Troth I was only —'

'Don't stand bletherin' there,' interrupted the other angrily. ' What 'll ye be doin' at Derry? '

'At Derry? He! he! he! That 's just fwhat I was tould not to let an to a livin' sowl, but there can be no harrum, musha, in tellin' a fine jintleman like yersilf now, kin there now? I 'm goin' to Derry for two hunner pund. That 's what I 'll be doin'. What do ye say to that? '

' An' who 'd give you two hundred pounds, ye cod ye? '

'Two hunner pun', he! he! he! two hunner pun' . . !'

' Look here, my good fellow, does this money belong to you? '

' Me is it? No for shure, it 's the masther's. '

' And who 's your master? '

' The masther? Troth he 's just the masther, he! he! he!'

' What 's his name, you idiot? '

' Oh his name, his name 's Misther O'Connor of Inniskilling.'

' And has he much money? '

' Lashins.'

' An' what did the master send you for? '

' Fwhat for? Two hunner pun', he! he! he!'

' Why did he choose you to send? Don't you

know that there is a highwayman on this road?'

'Ah, that's just it yer 'ahner, I'm only a fule, so the thafe of the wurruld won't suspect me, but mebbe I'll not be such a fule as he thinks me.'

'How do you know I'm not the highwayman?'

'Ah ye're makin' game yer 'ahner. A fine jintleman like yersilf on a splendacious baste, the likes of yon is it that would be a dhirty robber? I'm not such a fule as to think that.'

'Well, well, what would you do if you did meet the robber?'

'Rin like a hare, yer 'ahner.'

'That old horse of yours would n't, I'm thinkin'. And if ye could n't run?'

'Well, I dunno,' and Barney scratched his head — 'stan' I spose an' give him the money if he axed far it.'

'A nice cowardly thing to do with your master's property.'

'Betther be a coward nor a corp,' replied Barney pithily.

'Well, I hope you'll find Derry a good sort of place.'

'For sartin, shure. Why wud n't I? I hear

tell ye can git as much cahfee there for a pinny as wud make tay for tin min.'

'Will you shake your elbow?'

'Thank ye kindly, sirr, but niver a dhrain do I take.'

'Well, the loss is yours. Here's luck!' and the stranger raised the rejected flask to his own lips.

'Will you be coming back this way?'

'I dunno.'

'What day will you be coming back, d'ye think?'

'I d'no.'

'To-morrow?'

'Aiblins.'

'Well, will ye be coming back the day after?'

'Mebbe I might an' mebbe I might n't, an' mebbe I might too.' The omadhawn had turned suddenly sulky after the manner of his kind, and it was evident that there was nothing more to be got out of him. The stranger saw this, and said, 'Well, don't go telling everybody you meet all you've told me, and mind you don't get robbed before you get back here. Good luck to you.'

'Morrow till ye, an' God be wi' ye, where-ever ye go,' responded the haverel as he rode off.

Two days afterwards Barney was once more passing through the Gap, this time on his return journey. It was evening and the scene was very different from the first occasion of his visit to the place. Instead of damp and mist there was now brilliant sunshine which flooded the valley and the far hill-sides with purple light, and glittered upon the surface of the brook with the slanting rays of eventide. Barney could now see that the side of the precipice leading downwards from the road was not absolutely perpendicular, but was diversified with rocky ledges and huge boulders, which lent a wild and rugged aspect to the scenery, intensified by the great mountains which towered steeply upon either hand. While the sight of the sea in the background added to the loneliness of the mountains the vaster loneliness of the ocean.

At a turn of the road he came upon the stranger stationed at the same point as before, and as then drawn up across the path.

'Why it's yer 'ahner's self agin,' cried Barney delightedly, 'more power to yer elbow.'

'Oh, so you're here, then,' said the other with evident relief, 'where's the money?'

'The money is it? Troth it 's in my pooch safe enough, I 'll warrant, I thought I 'd sarcum-vint that robber villain.'

'Hand it over.'

'I hope yer 'ahner has n't met him yersilf at ahl.'

'Hand it over.'

'Hand what over? Is it me yer talkin' to, surr?'

'Yes, I want that money you 've got. I 'm the highwayman.'

'Now you 're jokin', surr,' said the natural anxiously. 'Shure ye would n't go to play a thrick that road upon a poor bhoy.'

'Don't stand jabberin' there, give me the hard stuff.'

'An' he was the thafe ahl the time, see that now, he! he! he!' and the idiot went into a fit of laughter, rocking himself to and fro on his horse, and wagging his hands helplessly.

'Give me the money, damn you,' said the robber out of patience as he drew a pistol from his holster, 'or I 'll shoot you.'

'Oh, wirra, wirra, shure yer 'ahner would n't harrum Barney, he 's only a nathral, that never done no one no hurt, may the saints presarve ye.'

'I don't want to hurt you,' said the other, 'but I must have that two hundred pounds, so just hand it over, and no more foolery.'

'Ah thin,' cried the idiot, flying into a passion, which lent fluency to his invective, 'bad cess to ye for a decaivin' sarpent, may the divil roast ye for yer blandandherin' ways, gettin' me saycrit fram me, an' thin thurnin' on me. Bad scran to yer sowl. My curse and the curse of Crummle rest on ye. Sorra till ye. May ye live till ye wish ye were dead, an' die like a dog in a ditch, but the divil a thraneen of the masther's wud ye get, if I had to throw it from here into the say, so now,' and before the robber could prevent him he had taken the two packages of money from his pocket and thrown them down the precipice.

'Ay, luk at it now, luk at the goold aleppin' an' arowlin' over the stones, there 's yer money, ye thafe ye, much good may it do ye.'

As he spoke the paper packages burst on the rocks below, and the glittering shower of coins could be seen leaping from point to point, ever gathering velocity, while the ring of the metal upon the stones mingled with the babbling of the brook, towards which they were hastening.

With a curse the robber replaced his pistol in its holster, leaped from his horse, and began scrambling down the cliff, to try and save a part of the spoil if possible.

'He! he! he!' laughed the idiot, as he rocked and swayed at the edge of the precipice, and he giggled and slobbered and gibbered, as he pointed at the robber toiling after his elusive quest.

When the highwayman was about half-way down the descent, Barney mounted the other's fine black horse and began to ride off, leaving his own old screw behind.

'Stop, damn your soul,' cried the highwayman, starting to climb up again. 'What are ye doin', ye jape ye? Stop, or I'll shoot ye.'

'Shute away, ye blatherskite,' replied Barney cheerfully, 'have n't I got yer pistols in yer own holsters? but I'm thinkin' I'm goin' to take this illigant baste of yer 'ahner's instid av me own. Shure, fair exchange is no robbery, an' ye can make up the differ in the price foreby the lucks-penny with all them bright farthin's down there. I got them out of the bank o' purpose for yous.'

After that day the highwayman was seen no more in his accustomed haunts. But in honor of the omadhawn's stratagem the place has ever since borne the name of Barney's or Barnesmore Gap.

'MORE CRUEL THAN THE GRAVE'

THERE were four of them, — two men and two girls, — and they sat on the top of the outermost cliffs of Donegal, dangling their legs over the Atlantic. Behind them stretched Donegal Bay, with its rugged, mountainous shores and varied inlets, the sun throwing purple shadows on the steep sides of Slieve League. In this direction they could see the long lines of towering black-faced cliffs, clad in parts with honeysuckle and capped with heather, giving place as they marched inland to lowland stretches, where the sandy dunes with their tufted bent-grass sloped gradually to the water's edge, from which they were separated by strips of hard and silvery strand. Looking out westward in front of them there was nothing but the wide ocean between them and America.

' Well, and how do you find your new parish, Fairchild?' said the elder of the two men, throwing a piece of rock-slate at a passing gull, 'slightly different from anything you ever came across in England, is n't it?'

'Yes, this is an entirely new experience for me. Of course six months is a very short time to justify a wholesale opinion, but I never imagined previously that quite such a primitive people could exist anywhere in these islands.'

The speaker was a young English curate, only recently appointed to this out-of-the-way parish of Kilcross. His companion was a young ship's doctor home on leave. The two girls were the granddaughters of the vicar, one of the few clergymen in Ireland who refused to commute at the time of the disestablishment of the Irish Church, and who now, at the advanced age of ninety, was still enjoying the fruits of his obstinacy. It could be seen from the bundles beside them that the girls were on their way to a bathe, when they had met the two men and fallen into conversation with them.

'Primitive is just the word to describe them,' replied the doctor, ' it is curious how utterly our civilization has passed them by in this remote corner of the world, and left them exactly the same as their earliest forefathers must have been generations back, A fisher folk are proverbially benighted, but shut in here between the seriousness of the barren soil on the one hand and the melancholy of the Atlantic upon the other, the inhabitants of these high-land villages upon the seaboard are utterly barbarous. And they possess all the virtues and vices of uncivilized types. Hospitable, good-natured, treacherous and superstitious, they have the unreflecting cruelty common to the child and the savage — I could tell you some horrible stories about that if I liked — joined to — what shall I call it? — their want of solidarity of character.'

'I don't quite understand, though you are saying things that I have often dimly tried to puzzle out for myself,' interrupted the elder girl.

'I suppose you refer to my last phrase, Miss Ruth. I mean that there is no common element running through their natures and joining their different moods and emotions together, harmo-nizing them or shading them off one into the other. There is no coherence about them, no

4

compromise, they are a mere medley of odd passions, all in the raw and without sequence, each following crudely and logically from its own peculiar premises. None of their moods ever has reference to any previous mood.'

'I suppose, Seymour,' said the clergyman thoughtfully, 'that is why I have found I could never get any grip of them. I have often thought I was progressing favorably, making an impression, and then at some sudden turn, as they express it themselves, I have "come a jundy up agin'" a blank-wall in their character, and had to confess myself baffled again.'

'Yes, that is it. I have been brought up among them and been familiar with them since childhood, and I can safely say that with the exception of Miss Ruth here, I have never known any one not of their own race and religion obtain any hold over them, or exercise the slightest effect upon their conduct in any one way, and even her influence stops short with the women. The difficulty is that there is no central point to work upon. There is no use trying to argue with them or soften them. One mood can only be exorcised by another. Their obstinacy or their superstition can only be cast out by an appeal to their cupidity or their fear. It is there that the hold of the Roman Catholic Church over them comes in. The priest has the power to excommunicate any one at any time, which means not only destruction for them in the next world, but also discomfort in this. We Protestants have no such deterrents. If you take my advice you won't remain here long. You don't sympathize enough with the people ever to understand them. They want a stern, determined, coarse-grained nature to drive them. You are too delicate and subtle for them. Your work is all thrown away here.'

'The people are not necessarily the only attraction,' returned the curate a little sullenly.

'Oh, do come and look at this wee bubbly bit,' broke in the younger girl, who, unlike her more mature and graver sister had ceased to pay any further attention to the conversation, as soon as she found that it had turned upon the 'Parish.'

'Just watch it,' she continued, pointing to a crevice in the rocks below, 'the water is ever so far away down, and then it rises gradually higher and higher until it reaches the edge with a "plop" and runs over, and then it sinks again right down until it leaves the long wrack at the sides hanging clear out of the water and dripping down into it like dead water snakes, till the next wave comes and flushes them into life again,' and she bobbed her head gravely in time with the rhythmical heave and subsidence of the recurrent surges, glinting the sunlight from her bright gold hair.

'Yes, that shows a very heavy swell. It is the distant muttering of a storm far out in the Atlantic. A bad sign for your bathe. In fact I don't think you ought to bathe at all to-day, Miss Selina. These ground-swells are very dangerous, and the sea looks angry to-day. Just notice how dirty and disturbed the water is with the sand stirred up from its depths. That fringe of seaweed too along the tidal mark is ominous.'

'Dangerous, nonsense,' replied the girl. 'Why, the sea is as calm as a mill-pond, and I never saw a lovelier day. You're becoming a perfect old woman, Dr. Seymour. I'm sure even Mr. Fairchild doesn't think it dangerous, now, do you?'

'It certainly appears calm enough to me,' said the person thus appealed to.

Seymour flushed and retorted shortly with a slight sneer.

' Fairchild does n't know the sea well enough to be afraid of it.   He speaks out of the depths of his ignorance.   But a wilful woman must have her way.   So I 'll leave you to your bathe. Good morning!' and the two men turned away along the top of the cliff, while the girls ran gayly down the sloping path that led to the little cove below.   They had not gone far before Seymour recovered from his temporary ill-humor, and halted.

' I 'm not easy in my mind about those girls,' he said.   ' A ground-swell like that is more treacherous than the nature of our Irish friends beyond.   I think we ought to wait here within earshot of them,' and they both sat down upon the sod bank with their backs to the sea.

For a time there was a moody silence, which the clergyman broke at last, enviously, kicking his heels against the sod ditch.

' Of course I 've got no chance against you. I can see that.   And I think it 's hardly fair.'

' Eh! why! what!' ejaculated the other, starting out of a reverie.

' That we are both in love with the same

girl. And what chance have I against a man
of the world like you, who has travelled and
studied human nature and womankind? I
think it's hardly fair,' repeated the youth with
what sounded suspiciously like a snivel.

'But I thought it was the sister you were
in love with.'

'Oh, nonsense. The sister's all very well
in her way. But no one could look at her
for a moment while the other one is by.'

'No, of course not,' assented Seymour with
conviction.

'She is so beautiful, so large and gracious
and serene.'

'That's not at all how I read it. Your
notion of her sounds very much like the character of — hark! what's that?'

A shrill long-drawn scream came pealing
towards them across the sea. They rose together and rushed tumultuously along the cliffs,
towards the sound, meeting another shriller
than the first as they ran. Suddenly they
burst into sight of the little cove, and halted
in surprise. So peaceful was the scene. The
sun was smiling broadly down upon an ocean
breathing the long deep respirations of a dream-

less slumber — couchant like a beast of prey.
In the foreground the two girls, clinging appre-
hensively together, were standing up to their
waist in water, their figures in the clinging
bathing gowns darkly silhouetted against the
muddy light green of the sandy-bottomed
bay.

But even as they gazed a silent treacherous
undulation passed like a breath across the naked
bosom of the sleeping ocean and crept stealthily
up to the terrified figures. Swiftly it lapped
their breasts and stole upwards about their
throats. And still it rose and rose with slow
remorseless volume, till it met softly above
their heads, leaving a few bubbles to mark the
spot where they had been. The giant swell
passed on its way, and for a moment they were
seen wallowing helplessly at large in the trough.
Then the back surge returned upon them and
swept them seawards.

'Good God, they'll be drowned,' cried Seymour, throwing off his coat. 'What are you
doing? You can't swim. Run as hard as you
can to the village for a boat. I'll do all that
can be done here.'

'Promise to save *her* at all costs.'

'Ay, I swear to that, though I and the other one should tread the short road to hell.'

The clergyman turned and ran vehemently away, his coat-tails flying in the breeze.

'Bring the priest with you if you can,' shouted Seymour after him, but a summer breath caught the words and wafted them away, and though the vague echo of them reached the runner's ears, their full import did not penetrate to his brain.

Reaching the village he quickly got a boat. The crew threw themselves into it, urged on by the women to 'be sure and save Miss Ruth.'

As soon as they rounded the horn of the bay a great throb of mingled joy and anguish gripped the young man by the throat. For a dripping figure was standing upon the shore and he knew that his love was saved — saved by his rival.

Midway between the boat and the shore was a small point of rock, to which the figure of the other girl could be seen clinging; so she too was safe. Beyond that again a swimmer's head was visible in the water. Directly they opened the point upon him, Seymour saw them, and, with a wave of his hand, turned wearily shorewards. The girl's eyes were bent on her rescuer away from the boat, and her numbed senses did not perceive the sound of the approaching oars. She thought herself abandoned, and, losing hope, released her hold and slipped off into the water. With a shout the boatmen dashed to her rescue.

For a few moments the bowman groped in the water with the boathook without success, but at last it caught in the girl's bathing dress and he drew her to the surface. The other men clustered around him and began to chatter in a low tone. The stroke, a man of huge stature called 'Big Dan Murphy,' sat stolidly opposite the curate, shutting out the view. As the men still chattered and made no further move Fairchild grew uneasy. Something in the harsher notes of their voices betokened a change of mood. That momentary check had been fatal, it had allowed their enthusiasm to cool and given an opening for more calculating thoughts.

'What are you doing, men? Lift her into the boat,' he said, and rising to his feet he saw for the first time the face supported just above the surface of the water. The face was the face of Ruth — Ruth whom he had thought safe on shore. 'My God, lift her in quick,' he repeated, with a tremor in his voice.

The men muttered together, looking at him askance. One of them spoke a few words in strident Erse to the stroke.

'What does he say, Dan?' the young man demanded impatiently.

'He says,' replied the other phlegmatically, 'that she's a corp ahlready, and that it will only bring bad luck to the fishin' to take a dead body intil the boat.'

'But she's not dead,' cried Fairchild wildly, 'she was alive this minute on the rock. Make them lift her in.'

'Ye shud ha' brought the priest wid ye,' responded the giant with a neutral compassion; 'them wans is not to be druv by no man barrin' him, when they jine to take a conthrairy notion yon road.'

At this the echo of Seymour's last words returned clearly upon Fairchild's brain, and he cursed himself for his inattention. With it, too, there returned the remembrance of other words of Seymour's. He recognized that this was a crisis and braced himself to make a fight of it.

' Good God, men,' said he, ' you don't mean
to say you will let a woman die before your
eyes for a miserable superstition like that?
Why, I can see her breathe; she's as much
alive as any of us.   See, she's opening her
eyes.   For God's sake lift her in,' he broke off,
in frenzied tones.   They turned indifferently
away, and the hopelessness of pulling against
the dead weight of their superstition settled
down over his mind and enveloped it in black
despair.   But he continued desperately:

' If you take her in I 'll give you money, — a
hundred pounds a head, — five hundred pounds,
— I 'll give you all that I 've got.'   For a
moment their attention was attracted and their
cupidity aroused.   But the sums he mentioned
were so large that they defeated his own object.
They conveyed no meaning to the narrow
minds of the fishermen accustomed to think
in pence.   They sounded in their ears like
promises of fairy gold.   Had he offered them a
new boat and nets they would have understood
it and jumped at the offer.   But he paid the
penalty now of not knowing his ground.   Once
more they turned away.

Then something went snap in his temple,

and he lost control over himself, and with that all chance of influencing them.

' You are not men,' he raved, the tears streaming from his eyes, ' but brutes.   It is too cruel. You can't mean it.   Will no one help me? I 'll have you all hung for murdering her.   Why haven't I got a pistol with me? and I 'd shoot you all like dogs.   You hounds, I 'll strangle you now,' and he threw himself choked with sobs upon the stroke.   But it was not more hopeless to cast his puny force against the dead wall of their superstition than against that iron chest.   The giant took him in his arms like an infant, and replaced him gently upon his seat. The others laughed.

' Av the whelp does n't quit bletherin', putt him in the wather along of his swateheart, Dan,' said one of them in an ugly tone.

The young man rose again from his seat, and tried to cast himself over the side, even though he could n't swim, to be beside his beloved. But again he was caught and placed on the thwart, to which this time he was strapped down, so that mercifully he could not see over the gunwale of the boat.

Then the men tied a rope round the girl's

arms, dropped her calmly into the water again, resumed their oars, and rowed sullenly back the mile to the village. Behind them the body spun at the end of its long rope. In the stern-sheets curses and blasphemies bubbled from the lips of a gibbering maniac.

When they reached the shore, not only was life extinct, but both the girl's arms were broken. The sea itself would have been more merciful than that.

. . . . . .

When Fairchild awoke from his long bout of brain fever his eyes fell upon Seymour.

' Why did n't you save her as you promised? ' were the first words he uttered.

' Nonsense, old man, you 're wandering still. Of course I saved her. You forget, it was her sister Ruth that those devils murdered.'

' Oh, it 's all a horrible mistake,' groaned the invalid, as he buried his face in his hands and turned his head to the wall, moaning like a wounded thing in pain.

THE AIR–GUN

IT was Philip Brandon's last day at Oxford.
Behind him lay four pleasant years spent partly
in · dawdling through the Honors schools,
chiefly in gratifying his own various tastes for
athletics, social intercourse, and contemporary
literature.   In front of him lay — what?   The
thought stuck in his throat; so, in an unsettled
spirit, he lit a cigar and sauntered out into the
High, with a vague idea of doing the rounds
as he used in his schoolboy days, and taking
a last farewell of the old city's ' coronal of
towers.'

Passing a gunsmith's, he remembered he
wanted some cartridges, and, going in to buy
them, saw there that fatal air-gun, which he
afterwards declared to himself was the cause
of all his troubles.   Curiously enough this
shirking of the responsibility of his own acts
was not in his case a sign of weakness, it was

his very directness of mind that made him perceive and value the morality of his own conduct with the same remorseless logic as he extended to his neighbors, and would have made him intolerable to himself had he not taken refuge in some such obliquity of mental vision. A man who is free from self-deception is not a man at all, but a monster. Self-hypocrisy, after all, is only another form of self-respect, and it is part of human nature to desire our own good opinion no less than other people's.

To outward seeming the air-gun was merely an ordinary hazel walking-stick with a crook handle, and the closest examination would barely reveal its real nature. In his restless mood this novelty in puzzles took Brandon's fancy, and he bought it on the spot. There was something sinister and secret about having this unsuspected weapon. He was pleased with it, as he had been pleased when a boy with his first sword-stick; and he determined then and there to tell no one that it was more than it actually appeared — an ordinary walking-stick.

He had packed all his luggage and ware-

housed his furniture in readiness for his start to
Ireland in the morning, so there was nothing
left to be done but to wonder why he was going
there at all.   His uncle had hitherto paid his
way through school and college, but had recently told him that his income had been so
diminished by the depreciation in Irish land,
that he could no longer afford to continue his
allowance or start him in a profession, as he
had originally intended; so that, on leaving the
'Varsity, Philip must shift for himself, but
would be welcome, if he chose, to come on a
visit while ' looking about him. '

This invitation Philip had accepted, though
without much feeling of gratitude to his uncle.
He felt that he had been hardly used.   He had
been led to expect a fair start in a profession;
and now, at an age when most other avenues
of employment were closed to him, with a useless general education and no means of supple-
menting it with a special one, he was calmly
turned adrift.   It would have been kinder to
have cast him off earlier, when his tastes were
still unformed and his notions less refined.
Even now he could not help feeling that it
would only have taken a slight effort on his

uncle's part to redeem the tacit pledges he had given; but with all his easy good-nature, the old man had the failing, which so often goes with it, of intense selfishness, and had no idea of curtailing his own pleasures in order to set his nephew upon his legs. It would do the young man good, he thought, to knock about a little at the outset. But he had made a mistake: Philip's nature was too intense to take kindly to such discipline, it was apt to strike in too deeply, and there was no knowing what the result might be. As it was, Oxford had performed its part for him, as for so many other penniless young men, of totally unfitting him for any professions but the pulpit and the birch-rod, the two which his soul most utterly abhorred.

Perhaps it would have been wiser under these circumstances to have started work at once, but Philip felt a desire to take breath before his plunge into the stream of life. Hitherto his life had been a series of preparations for some one definite event, — his examinations, the end of his school life, the end of his university life. Now he had come to the end of the latter, and he found that it was not an end nor even a beginning. The whole of life lay spread before him to choose from, with no means of making a choice. Contemplating it in the mass, the boundless indefiniteness of the prospect bewildered his gaze and paralyzed his energies. The world was so large he did not know where to begin upon it. He was not close enough to it to recognize that there, as elsewhere, only a single stage of the journey occupies our attention at a time. He shrank aghast into himself and took refuge in habit. His habit led him to his uncle's house.

Arrived in the cheerful island of his birth, what with the dampness of the climate, and the dulness of country life at Lisnamore, his lassitude grew upon him and enveloped him as with a miasma. He was always a great reader, and now did little else but read novels. Real life pressed so heavily upon him, that he was driven to take refuge in a world of unrealities. But they increased rather than diminished his malady. This cloud of alien personalities obscured his own, acting upon his mind like an anæsthetic, so that for weeks he lived and moved in that atmosphere of unreality which constant novel-reading engenders, and which is so apt to unfit one for the stress of actual life. A melancholy and moodiness of humor possessed him, so that he passed whole days with scarcely speaking a word, and to the other inmates of the house he appeared a very different person from the light-hearted and good-natured lad of former visits.

In fact, up to this point in his life the easy good-nature common to the rest of his family had been his most salient characteristic upon the surface, and he had taken for granted that it was part of his real nature. So long as the world had treated him kindly he had met it in his turn with a most amiable countenance. It is true that he had not been widely popular at college, but he had explained this to himself by ascribing it to too great self-reliance on his own part. His epithets for his own character in the secret places of his heart were ' strong ' and ' original ' — epithets which he had justified to a certain extent at Balliol by going his own way irrespective of Dons and lectures, and by a certan readiness to act without reference to conventional standards or traditions, together with a disdain for the ordinary grooves of life, which made his conduct under any given circumstances difficult to foretell. Nevertheless, he had been liked by his own set; and when he did go out of his way to cultivate an acquaintance, perhaps partly owing to this very fastidiousness of his, he rarely failed to attract.

But now that his lot had become soured, he surprised himself at times indulging in moods and fancies, that showed him there were unsuspected forces in his nature which had hitherto lain dormant, but which might spring into activity at any instant. In his moments of introspection he sometimes dimly wondered now if he were not in truth just a little bit selfish at bottom, else how to account for this extravagant solicitude about his own fortunes.

The fact was that the unsettlement of the conditions of his existence, the gravity of this first appearance of his upon the platform of every-day life, and the dreariness of the outlook had affected his nature more deeply than he was himself aware. His life at Oxford, with its atmosphere of ease and luxury, had unfitted him for the stern realities of the world in which he was now called upon to earn his bread. The hopelessness in modern life of effecting one's aim had thus early begun to impress him.

Nowadays, as heretofore, he saw that effort is not wasted, but that it produces a result absurdly inadequate to the force expended. Everywhere around him he saw men of brilliant parts and dauntless courage ground beneath the wheels of that modern Juggernaut, the soul-destroying round of mechanical toil; men whose ambition originally would not have strained at kingdoms, reduced to hack writers for journals and ushers in a school. A young man aims at the moon and hits a suburban cottage. Pegasus is put to grind a mill. Seeing all this, he felt shut-in upon every side. For a time he beat the pinions of his mind helplessly against his prison-bars. Then the black moodiness of despair enwrapped him in its folds. He had no tools with which to shape his destiny, so he apathetically left the issue upon the knees of Fate.

But he was young and buoyant, and this depression could not last forever. The first sign of its breaking up was a desire for outdoor exercise. He roused himself from his lethargy, and to escape its influence determined on a fishing excursion to a distant mountain lough. He thought that the drive and the fresh air would re-invigorate him. And indeed by the time he had accomplished the twelve miles there, and had caught a few trout, he was more like his usual self; but by noon the weather had settled down into one of those broiling days which one occasionally meets with in Ireland, generally in October, and fishing had become hopeless. The fish were small, but plentiful, and now they rose all round him, and flapped his flies with their tails in a tantalizingly derisive manner.

He had brought his air-gun with him, and to while away the time, he got it out and began shooting at the fish as they rose. He soon found that, by allowing for the curve of the pellets, he could hit a spot the size of half-a-crown at a dozen yards with some certainty, and at this sport he amused himself for the rest of the afternoon, until he had acquired a fair command of the weapon. Gradually as he continued his pastime, the vicious snick of the bullets in the water infected his blood, and gave rise to curious thoughts within him. He grasped his weapon more tightly, the perspiration stood out upon his forehead, and a fierce satisfaction surged through him each time he hit his aim.

Suddenly he came to himself with a start and recognized the emotion that had been driving him. It was a feeling of murderous revolt against that society which had given him expensive tastes without the means of gratifying them. All those yearnings of his for fine books and pictures, the pleasures of the palate, and the love of women, for everything which can be bought by money, or, rather cannot be procured without its possession, must run to waste and remain forever unsatisfied. It was against the possessors of all those good things which he had not and could never hope to have, that in his mind he had been directing those bullets with such fatal accuracy.

The knowledge came home to him with a sudden shock, and horror-stricken at himself he hastily put up his rod and started on his homeward journey. The sultriness of the day, as is often the case in the hour before sunset, had become even intensified. There was not a breath of air, as he jogged quietly along in the evening light. All nature seemed to perspire, and a dull yellow haze covered the surrounding country. The road stretched straight and dusty before him between its walls of sod;

and upon either hand spread a flat and unin-
teresting expanse of bog and moorland. The
approach to the town was signalled by the
change from the clay to a limestone soil; and
instead of the occasional ditches of sod or huge
drains, which divided the country and restricted
the wanderings of a few isolated cows and
donkeys, frequent stone walls began to appear,
built by piling odd stones together without
cement of any kind, and separating fields of
hay, wheat, and potatoes.

Rather more than half the distance had been
traversed, when an object detached itself from
the haze in the middle distance and rapidly
approached. As it drew near he saw that it
was a car, with a man sitting upon one side,
and the other side turned up; and as it came
still closer he recognized in the driver a cousin
of his own, the land-steward of the Duke of
Ulster. The other was going to pass with a
wave of his whip. But a sudden revulsion of
feeling had come over Philip. Nature had
taken upon herself the oppression of his own
spirits, and had shamed him out of his febrile
emotions by the spectacle of her larger melancholy. So now that he had met a fellow-

creature he was glad to escape the surrounding monotony and was seized with a sudden craving for conversation.

'Hullo, Dick, whither away so fast?' he shouted. 'Here, have I not seen you for a whole year, and you cut me as dead as if you owed me money.'

Both pulled up their horses, and Dick replied: 'Sorry, old man. Did n't mean to offend you, but I 've got a lot of money here, so I 'm in a hurry to get home, and have it off my hands. Been collecting the quarter's rents, and have got about five thousand pounds in cash to take care of.'

'Pooh, you 're codding. Why did n't you put it in the Bank?'

'Could n't. Shuts early on Saturdays. And no safe in my office to keep it in.'

'Well, but after all there would n't be so much harm done, even if you did get it collared. I suppose you 've taken the numbers of the notes.'

'Why, my dear fellow,' replied the other, all the tenants are small farmers, and pay either in coin or in one pound notes, that would be just as difficult to trace.'

So saying he put his horse into a walk to pass him. At that moment feeling for his whip, Philip's hand fell upon that demon-possessed air-gun, which he had left loaded on the cushion beside him. An electric thrill passed through all his nerves. Almost without volition the weapon flew to his shoulder. He saw Dick's temple turned sideways towards him for a moment. There was a whip-like crack, a thud, and his body swayed heavily and fell backwards on the stone ditch beside the road. Both horses stood still. All nature held her breath. A vast silence brooded over the landscape. There wasn't a figure to be seen within the horizon.

He sat there quite still for at least five minutes, still grasping his infernal instrument. He did not realize at first what had happened, and waited for Dick to rise up again. It was as though something outside himself, that did not belong to him, had done this thing. His murderous thoughts of the forenoon had borne unexpected fruit. Presently Dick's horse began to crop the grass by the wayside. The crunching sound broke in upon his stupefaction. Dick himself did not move. He got down and walked up to him, keeping carefully on the grass all the way, so as to leave no trace of footsteps. He had fallen with the back of his head upon a stone, and even to Philip's inexperienced eye it was evident that he was already dead. He had not expected this, but it was better so. He felt his heart, to make sure. It had stopped beating.

Then he got on the car to search for the money. First he looked in the well. It was not there. A cold perspiration burst over him. What if Dick were only joking after all? But soon he found the bag under the end of the cushion his cousin had been sitting on. He started off the horse with a lash of the whip, which he laid down again beside the dead man, rolled a large stone into the middle of the road to account for the accident, carried the bag to his own car, wrapped it in his mackintosh, and quickly drove on home.

At first his faculties had been stunned with a physical numbness by the sudden shock of his own action, and everything that he had done hitherto had been merely mechanical. But now his mind began to recover its tone. It rushed at once to the other extreme of an almost painfully intense activity. Thoughts whirled through his head at lightning speed. In one illuminating flash he saw himself in his naked reality. His seething ambition, his easy-going temper, his constitutional dislike of running in grooves, and his recent despondency, all rose and confronted him in the guise of a colossal Egoism, a selfishness which desired exemption from the common lot of mankind, a lot of hopeless futureless toil; while a yet darker suggestion loomed dimly forth from the background of his mind. He recognized that his good-nature at ordinary times was really only an absolute indifference to other people's affairs, except when they touched him nearly. Even in his own concerns his cold logicality of intellect kept him supine except in cases of the extremest importance. This was really the first important crisis of his life. He had in a measure that habit of self-analysis, which goes with a cold and self-centred brain, though it was chiefly of the flattering sort, and he knew that his nature was of an almost elemental simplicity and directness; but he had rarely suspected before to-day that when deeply stirred an elemental cruelty was one of its ingredients.

These moments of self-revelation come in the life of all of us, when our ordinary every-day self, familiar to ourselves and our home circle, is suddenly brought face to face with that other deeper lying and often semi-barbarous self, which crouches hidden beneath the veneer of civilization and the mask of social habit, and we are forced into a swift mental comparison of the two. Happy is the man in whom these two selves are identical; for his shall be a stagnant life, and is not that the life of the gods? But these flashes of insight do not remain long with us. We make haste and cover them up, and put such importunate thoughts away from us, and only a vague uncomfortableness remains in the memory for a short time.

So in Philip's mind the first clearness of the impression of his own baseness soon faded, and was swallowed up in consideration of its consequences. His act, that concrete expression of his character, could not be glossed over. It remained behind there in all its naked hideousness in the person of his murdered cousin lying in the road.

Questions of expediency came first. Could he risk finding the body and taking it home with him? It was not yet too late. No, the money would prevent that, though otherwise it might be the best plan. There was only the one road and he must have met his cousin somewhere. But he had almost walked his horse hitherto, it was still quite fresh, and now if he drove hard, he could say that he had met Dick two or three miles nearer home, and the time would agree all right. And the money? It might very well appear that some tramp had come by and taken it, after the accident had occurred. For himself — offenders that did not belong to the ordinary criminal classes, were always detected through their own folly. They could n't control their countenances, or were overcome by remorse or betrayed the hiding-place of their spoil through over-anxiety. He had no such weaknesses. His education had at least done him the service of eradicating from his breast all scruples of conscience and superstitious fancies. He would conceal his gains in a safe spot he knew, and leave the country, so that he could not rouse suspicion. Next year he could return for the money, and it would go hard with him, but it would help him on the road to fortune.

He was ambitious. He had felt that he had ability above the ordinary. But the world had afforded him no opening. Now with five thousand pounds to back him the world was at his feet. He would select a congenial profession, which should draw forth all his energies, and would gain experience. Brains, experience, capital, each was almost useless by itself. But with a combination of the three what could he not do? The world was his oyster, and what he had been pining for latterly was the lack of an oyster-knife to open it.

Then Dick again! His thoughts reverted to him, poor chap! What of him? — how had it all come about? How had he come to do what he had done? Of course, in the first instance, it was the result of the opportunity of the moment and what he now saw to be his morbid craving after wealth for the last few weeks, the unhealthy dreams of a sick imagination. But to probe deeper. He was a fatalist, and it was no good crying over spilt milk. But let him at least be honest with himself; let him know the full meaning of his own action. Did he regret what had happened? would he do the same if he had to do it over again? Probably not; simply because in spite of the philosophers a man never does act twice alike under the same circumstances. But he felt that he would not have restored his cousin to life now, had that been possible. His main feeling was a guilty satisfaction that things had fitted in so well. He was not a coward, and before this the thought of suicide had come to him as a way out of his perplexities. For he had no near relations to think of, no ties to bind him to life. The worst that could now happen to him was almost preferable to the mediocre existence of mean and monotonous drudgery, which had formerly seemed his only prospect.

But gradually, as he brooded over the events of the afternoon, he began to lose sight of the benefit which had accrued to him. The idea had already become familiar by assimilation, and now his thoughts tended to dwell rather upon the danger which he had incurred, and whose proportions increased the longer he regarded it. A vague sense of irritation and injury began to grow up in his mind against his cousin as the author of his trouble, and even against the inanimate instrument of his violence, ' It's all the fault of that air-gun,' he muttered; and again, ' What business had he to meet me in the mood I was in with his babbling confidences? He has only himself to thank for his fate, and he has put my neck in danger too by his folly. Damn him!'

At the thought a sudden passionate wave of hatred, roused by the prick of personal fear, surged through his bosom. He was already beginning to set a higher value on life than heretofore, and he hated Dick that he had brought him the danger along with the benefit. He felt that he was unreasonable, but that only made him hate his cousin the more. After all, he had never seen much of Dick, and he was always a fool; he showed that even in his death — snuffed out like a candle. If it had been he, he would have made a harder fight for it than that; there was something contemptible about giving in so easily.

By this time he had reached the house. He carried the bag in under the mackintosh, and the walking-stick in his hand. The latter he put in the stand. He had used it constantly of late, and its absence would excite remark. The bag he wrapped in oil-cloth to keep it

6

from the damp, carried it out into the garden at the first opportunity, and hid it in an apple-tree, high up among the branches, in a hole, which had been his secret alone since boyhood.

Late that night the rumor reached the house that his cousin had fallen off his car and broken his neck. They all scouted the idea, and Philip mentioned having met him that afternoon a couple of miles out of the town, but Dick wouldn't stop to speak to him. The next day the rumor was confirmed: Philip had been the last person to see him alive.

For himself, Philip was physically prostrated, he could hardly move, and ached in every limb and every muscle: the fatigue resulting from the emotions which had racked him on the previous day was so much greater than any mere bodily fatigue he had hitherto known. The day afterwards — the Monday — he received a visit from the police-sergeant. He went cheerfully down. It was to summon him, he supposed, as a witness at the inquest, which was fixed for the morrow. Judge, then, of his surprise when he was arrested on a charge of having murdered his cousin.

He was very angry at first. Then the ab-

surdity of the situation struck him, and he
laughed aloud. Here had this lumbering
country lout stumbled on the truth by accident,
where a cleverer man would not have dreamt
of looking for it. But it might prove no laughing matter for him, once the scent had been
struck. The sergeant had applied, it seemed,
to the magistrate for the warrant, upon his own
responsibility, on the strength of a rumor that
Philip was at the bottom of the affair somehow.
How the rumor originated he never discovered
— probably from some distortion in the repetition of his own story of the meeting. But it
made matters very unpleasant for him for the
time. He said that he would go quietly to the
police-barracks if he were not handcuffed.

When he arrived there, the officer in charge —
the District Inspector, and an old friend of
Philip's, named Fitzgerald — cried out:

' Hullo, young 'un, what have you been doing
now? — run in for being drunk and disorderly?'
He thought that Philip had dropped in to see
him, and that the presence of the sergeant was
only a coincidence. Great was his surprise
when he heard that the young man was really
a prisoner — and upon what charge? He was

more angry than Philip had been, and called
the sergeant a blundering idiot, only in stronger
language. At last he cooled down again and
said:

'Well, never mind, you'll have to stop here
to-night, but you'll be let loose again to-
morrow, and everybody will think it only a
good joke.'

'Yes, that's all very well,' replied Philip;
'but Richards, the coroner, has a grudge against
me. As you know, he is the town baker; last
year he set up a carriage, and heard me call
it the bread-cart. He is sure to seize the
opportunity of taking the change out of me.
And I entirely fail to see where the joke comes
in.'

When he arrived in the court next day,
everybody was talking and laughing. They
thought it an absurd farce that he should be
accused of such a crime at all. Even the
police-sergeant had been sneered out of his
momentary inspiration of shrewdness long ago.
Philip alone knew what a hair's-breadth removed from earnest the affair was capable of
proving. He was like a man sitting on a powder
magazine with people ignorantly letting off

crackers all round him, one of which might at any moment blow him into eternity.

The body of the court was crowded as usual with corner-boys — a shiftless race of loafers peculiar to Ireland, who hang about the streets and the corners of the public-houses, and never do a day's work from year's end to year's end. They sponge upon their wives, spending all the money that they can beg upon drink during that short portion of the year that they are not retained in jail at their country's expense. ' God presarve yer ahner, wherever ye may go,' cried one of these as he entered. Philip had given him many a screw of tobacco, and knew that it was not for him, but for the loss of his tobacco that the man feared.

That bit of smartness about the bread-cart cost him an anxious time. The doctor gave his evidence that there were two injuries upon the body of the deceased — a cut upon the back of the head, which had been caused by falling off the car onto a stone, and a very small bruise on the temple. What had occasioned the latter, or if it were connected with the accident, he could n't say. But neither injury was sufficient to cause death. That had resulted from stoppage of the heart's action, which had long been diseased. Philip paid little attention to this; he was sufficiently honest with himself to recognize that he had committed murder in intention if not in actual fact.

Then the coroner wanted to know could the bruise on the temple have been caused by a blow from a whip or a stick? The doctor thought not. Nevertheless Philip's whip and all his sticks were fetched. The servants gave evidence as to the one he had used that day; it was handed round. Everybody was surprised at its lightness. Philip's heart stood in his mouth. The doctor and the coroner examined it minutely. If either of them had a grain of penetration, he was a lost man; but he could reckon with confidence on their stupidity. The air-gun preserved its secret well; for once it did not betray him. Its lightness proved even in his favor. The doctor decided that it was incapable of inflicting a stunning blow, that it was probably hollow, and would break on slight provocation.

He was acquitted, a verdict of accidental death returned, and the jury remarked severely upon the hasty action of the sergeant in adding to his natural grief at his cousin's death by such an unnatural accusation.

But Philip was in a fever until that wretched air-gun should be safely disposed of. At any moment it might change its mind and inform against him. He hooked his arm in Fitzgerald's directly the inquest was over, and said, ' Come along, and have a bathe after this beastly stuffy court; and as you have the custody of my sticks, I suppose you won't mind letting me have one now?' Fitzgerald laughed, and he took the air-gun. The other wanted to look at it, and see if it was really as light as they all made out. But Philip was not such a fool; the officer's trained eyesight was likely to prove too sharp.

They went to bathe in the river channel, a couple of miles below the town, and about half a mile from its mouth. When they had undressed, Philip threw the stick as far as he could into the middle, under pretence of sending Fitzgerald's retriever in after it. But the tide was on the ebb and the stream ran strong, so, as he knew would be the case, the dog turned back long before he reached the stick. Philip hoped never to see the wretched thing again. Suddenly a terror seized him; he could not leave it to the mercy of blind chance like that.   What if the sea gave up its prey? — the next tide might wash it ashore again.   Some one might find it and return it again, or worse still, find out the secret.   He must get rid of it more effectually at all hazards.   He plunged in after it, and quickly reached it; then pretending to put his feet between his hands, while holding the stick at either end he snapped it in two and cast it from him.

Meanwhile he had not noticed that he had rounded the last turn in the channel in its journey seaward.   He had got into the strength of the current, and it swept him away like a leaf.   He swam against it aslant with all his strength, but could not reach the edge, and in a moment he was among the breakers on the bar.

For a short time he succeeded in swimming over the waves or diving through them, and hoped to be able to get right out to sea.   But soon he was seized by a huge roller, the ninth wave, and carried resistlessly back again upon its crest.   The edge of the breaker curled thin beneath him like a shaving, dissolving into spray.   He looked down as he reached the bar, and suddenly the water seemed to vanish under him. One moment he was ten feet in the air, the next he fell with stunning force upon the sand, covered only with a couple of feet of surf. Before he recovered his senses, the broken water of the next wave was upon him, and the black-surge of the first was fighting with it for him. He was rolled over and over. Sand entered his eyes, mouth, nostrils, and ears. He was conscious of swallowing oceans of water. He struggled blindly for a time; he, at any rate, would not give in until the last gasp. But gradually there stole over him a feeling of drowsiness, of disinclination for further effort, a feeling that Fate had been too much for him. ' It's all that damned air-gun's fault,' he muttered again obstinately; and the waters closed over him.

When he came to himself again, he was lying on the strand, and Fitzgerald was bending over him. He had been washed by chance into the corner of an eddy near the shore, the D. I. had run along the bank, rushed in and rescued him before the life was quite buffeted out of him.

' Thanks, old boy,' he said, looking up at his friend; ' you have saved my life, and I won't forget it.'

'Oh, nonsense; you would do as much for me any day.'

They dressed in silence. At last Philip remarked:

'That stick was hollow after all; it snapped like a twig in my hands. I suppose it will fill with sand now and stop at the bottom of the sea.'

'Yes; you will never see it again, and a good job too: it was near being the death of you.'

'Yes,' said Philip, with a slow smile; 'it was very near being the death of me.'

THE GIANTS' CASTLE

'WILL you come out with me on revenue duty to-day, and try some still-hunting?'

The speaker was the District Inspector of police at Lisnamore, where I was spending my Long, as usual, some years ago. He was almost the only civilized being within miles of us, and as I discovered he hailed from the same public school as myself, we soon struck up an acquaintance and saw a great deal of each other.

On the present occasion, however, I hesitated a moment before accepting his invitation. The fact was, that it was his duty to search for illicit whisky, and only part of his ordinary routine, so that no one would think any the worse of him for doing it. But it was not mine: I was very good friends with the peasantry all about, and did n't wish to make myself unpopular by interfering with their making 'a sup of putcheen,' when they liked. On the other hand there was n't the least chance of our finding any just then. The priests had lately taken a dislike to the practice of the illicit trade as having a deteriorating influence on their flock, and had preached a crusade against it, and, what the police had been utterly powerless to effect for years, they had accomplished in a couple of months. To an Irishman it is a positive temptation to break the law — what else is it for? But to disobey the priests, at the risk of his soul's damnation, is quite another thing. So the convictions had dwindled immediately, Fitzgerald told me, from twenty a week to none at all, at which he was not a little chagrined, as besides being a sarcasm on the efficacy of the civil as opposed to the religious arm, the cessation of confiscations had deprived him of a source of income in the royalty upon captures.

Under these circumstances it could n't be much harm to accompany him upon his rounds. It only meant walking a certain number of miles through the surrounding bogs and mountains with a chance of an occasional shot, so I said, ' All right, wait till I get my gun and some cartridges, and I 'm with you,' and we set off.

The construction of these private stills is

primitive in the extreme, as they consist almost
entirely of a coil of copper piping called à
'worm,' for distilling the fermented barley. This
is boiled, and, passing through the 'worm,' which
is placed in a tub of cold water, the steam comes
out at the other end raw spirit: the operation is
repeated a second time to increase the strength
of the brew. The potheen thus made, is, like
all pure spirit, a colorless liquid. But, when
desired, it is colored by the simple process of
taking a red-hot poker and a lump of sugar-candy
and dropping the burnt sugar into the whisky
until the required tinge is reached.

The most usual method of concealing the
still when not in use is to choose a lonely part
of the mountain, cut a circular piece out of the
sod large enough to sink a barrel, containing
the plant, and then replace the sod. This hiding-
place is called by the peasantry a ' coach,' probably from some corruption of the French
cache, and the only means of discovering its
secret is that a trained eye can detect the
very slight difference between the color of
the turf on the circular patch and the grass
around it. So, as may be imagined, it is
possible to walk a good many miles and

pass a good many stills without making any discovery.

Sometimes the barrel is concealed by sinking it at the end of a piece of rope into a mountain lough; to the rope a thick piece of string is attached; to that a thinner piece; to that again a piece of thread, which is fastened round an ordinary bottle-cork. To recover the barrel, it is necessary first to find the cork, and then to haul up the lengths of increasing thickness until the original rope is reached. Of course it is a hopeless task for any one not acquainted with the exact spot of concealment to try and find one of these corks except by tracking the owner.

An instance has even been known, when the barrel was sunk in the middle of a highway, and the road levelled over it to look the same as usual; a quick-eared policeman, however, noticed the hollow sound as he drove over the place, and earned the praises of his superiors and the curses of the owners by unearthing a fine cask of malt.

Fitzgerald and I were not so lucky; the only bag we made was a few hares and snipe, and to get these we walked upwards of thirty miles.

We had six of Fitzgerald's policemen with us
to help in our search, fine long-legged men like
all the members of the force.   The D. I. himself was considerably the smallest of the company, for naturally the standard is not so high
for the officers as for the ordinary rank and file.
So for the first fifteen miles he was clean out
of it in walking powers, but every mile after that
length of stride told for less and stamina for
more, and by the end of the day Fitzgerald
with his long back and duck legs had· walked
us all to a standstill.

Our way lay across wild mountainous slopes
clad in heather, varied by swampy patches
where the rushes grew thickly, and studded
with large boulders.   Spread out on either
side of us the policemen made a fine line of
beaters, which roused every living thing before
us that there was to rouse.   To tell the truth
we did not take the trouble to look for much
else, knowing it hopeless, and my adventures
did not begin until the business of the day
was over.

It was in the evening on our return that
we struck the coast a couple of miles from
home, near the Giants' Castle.   This was an

old ruin, built on a projecting headland, con-
cerning which the legends current in the
country-side were more numerous than I could
mention. That dearest to the minds of children
and the simple peasantry about was embodied
in its name, and had its origin in the Cyclo-
pean nature of the masonry that yet remained.
Another account had it that this was one of
the castles of the O'Donnells, the ancient kings
of Ulster, while yet later stories described its
inhabitants as smugglers, who had run many
a valuable cargo at this out-of-the-way spot.

The Castle was built on an immense slab
of rock which completely overhung the sea,
and a feature in all the legends was the existence of a well at the outermost corner of
the building, which was bored clean through
the solid rock with a perpendicular drop into the
sea beneath. In the legends of the Giants
they had used this well as a rubbish hole for
the bones of the victims they had devoured;
by the O'Donnells it had been employed as
a means of escape in time of danger; while
it was through its cavity that the smugglers
had raised their goods from the boats below.
The champions of each account clinched their

several legends with the triumphant argument,
'an' av ye don't believe me, ye can go an'
see far yersilf av the well is n't there,' which
of course was irrefutable.

Well, to return to my story, I wanted a
specimen of the large black-backed gull to
stuff, and thought this a good opportunity of
getting one. It was their habit to come in
round the cliffs at sunset, and the well, which
was now choked with rubbish, would make
a very good place to lie in wait for them;
there was a breach in the walls just at the
corner where it was situated, which would
afford an opening for a shot when the birds
came opposite to me, while I should be completely concealed from them.

Fitzgerald was hungry, so he went on home
with his policemen, and left me sitting in the
well. I was tired, and my moss-lined resting-
place proved so comfortable, that I fell asleep
almost immediately, and did n't wake until it
was already too dark to be able to see to shoot.

I started up, and was just going to clamber
out of the hole, when I heard the sound of voices
near me, and presently perceived that just
when I least expected it, I had come across

the owners of what was probably the last still in the country-side.

There were about a dozen men sitting in a group, evidently waiting to begin operations when it grew darker. It was even then too dark to see their faces, but I could tell by their voices they were all the worst characters of the neighborhood, most of them being fishermen belonging to that part of the coast.

Why I did n't go up to them at once and explain matters I really cannot tell, for I had nothing to fear from them. They all knew 'young Master Harry,' and under ordinary circumstances would not dream of doing me any harm, or think that I should do them any. But I suppose, remembering my occupation during the day, I had an uneasy conscience. Besides, the danger they ran of excommunication might render them rougher than usual. They certainly would not be pleased to see me there, while I could tell by their tones that they had already been partaking rather too freely of their own manufacture. If I stopped where I was they would never be any the wiser, as some scattered stones concealed me from them. I could tell from what they said that the 'coach' where they had their still hidden, was close at hand, and that they were going to fetch it soon; when they did, I could slip out and get away unperceived.

But my plans were upset by an unforeseen accident. Once or twice since I stood up in the well, I had heard a faint splash, as of earth or stones dropping into the sea beneath, and now of a sudden the ground under my feet gave way and disappeared with a sudden rushing sound. Instinctively I dropped my gun, which I have never seen since from that day to this, spread my arms out over each side of the hole, and was left dangling there with my feet over the abyss.

I was in no further danger from that source, as I could easily draw my body up onto the ground, but the sudden shock upset my nerve, and caused me to take the most unwise course possible in my position, one which I should never have chosen had I not been thus startled out of my presence of mind. I scrambled up onto the level ground, and as I saw the men coming towards me I dodged behind the outer wall of the ruin and ran off as hard as I could.

Of course they saw me almost immediately, and in a moment I had the whole crew yelling at my heels, making a clamor that sufficiently attested their condition. I had a pretty fair start, and at first my course lay along level ground. But presently I came to a dip, and I took the slope at a pace that would have made my reputation forever on the 'Varsity running-track.

But when I reached the bottom of the hollow I suddenly received a check. The ground disappeared from under my feet for the second time that day, and at the same instant rose up and hit me on the head. I felt stunned by the shock, which almost rent me in pieces, but had not time to indulge in luxuries just then, so without understanding exactly how I did it, I pulled the ground down over me again, and covered myself up not a moment too soon, as immediately afterwards I heard my pursuers tearing past my place of concealment. It was fortunate for me that the night was so dark, and their brains so muddled, that the fact of their not seeing me when they reached the top of the ridge did not rouse their suspicions, and they would go some way before they found they had lost me.

When I had time for reflection I discovered I was in the same hole with the smugglers' still. I had trod on the lid of the barrel which worked on a swivel in the middle, and as I pitched forward the opposite side had risen and caught me in the face; the wonder was it had not taken the head off me. Besides that my legs had fared badly amongst the smugglers' apparatus in the barrel, and my shins and their 'worm' had done about an equal amount of damage to each other.

As I lay there rubbing my bruises, I bitterly regretted the foolish impulse which had led me to take flight. If I had stood my ground at first, the fishermen's knowledge of me would have preserved me from the suspicion of spying on them and from consequent injury, but now that I had provoked these suspicions and fully roused the latent savagery of their natures, I could expect no better treatment than the merest stranger, if I were caught; while in their drunken state this chase after a human quarry would have such zest for them that they would not easily abandon it.

This thought roused me to action, for soon they would be coming back to the 'coach' for their still, and I should have grave reasons for fear if they found me there in the midst of the *débris* of their property.

I crawled out of the barrel at once, but even then I was too late, for already they were coming back and caught sight of me, and once again they were in full cry after me.

This time I had a better start, but I was crippled by the injuries I had received, and they gained upon me rapidly; to add to my troubles the shouts of my pursuers were answered by others who had been searching further afield and were now in front of me, and I found I was surrounded on all sides except towards the sea.

For a moment I was in despair, but suddenly a memory of my boyish days flashed across me, and I made straight for the cliffs. My pursuers thought they had me safe, and shouted with drunken glee, for the cliffs were fully two hundred feet in height and quite perpendicular.

I struck the top at almost exactly the spot I intended, and quickly found a narrow funnel-shaped ravine, down which I had often climbed to fish when a boy; but this time there was no leisure to climb. Digging my heels into the loose slack of the crumbling rock, and pressing my elbows against the sides of the chimney, I let myself go with a rush and roar of falling pebbles and slate, and arrived at the bottom minus all the skin on my elbows, ribs, and knees. But this bottom was in reality only a wide platform in a niche of the cliff half-way down its side, which, as it proceeded, dwindled into a narrow ledge on the face of the rock. Along this ledge I made my way, until I finally arrived at a point where there was a gap altogether of two or three feet in width, while the wall of the cliff overhung the place so closely that it was impossible to cross the break without going down on my hands and knees and crawling over it. This peculiarity had earned the ledge the name of ' the dog's pass ' amongst the few who knew of its existence, or would dare its perils for the sake of the rock-fishing to be had in the otherwise unapproachable cove below.

Once I had got to the further side of the gap I felt comparatively safe for the present, and, gathering some large stones, sat down a couple of yards from its edge; the break occurred at a projecting corner of the rock in such a position that any one on the other side of it could not see me until he had crawled across it.

Presently I heard the noise of rattling stones, which told me that one or more of my pursuers were descending the gully, but more cautiously than I had done, and then came the sound of shuffling footsteps along the ledge. There was a pause for a couple of minutes, before a large hand was laid on my side of the gap; I promptly dropped a rock upon it, and with a yell and a volley of curses it was rapidly withdrawn.

After that I knew my citadel was safe from attack in that quarter as there was a drop of over a hundred feet from the ledge onto the naked rocks beneath, which, even in the condition they were in, none of the smugglers would be very anxious to face. But I also knew that it was only a question of time, until they fetched a boat from the adjacent village, and took me in the rear from the side of the sea.

With a view to that event the sooner I was off the ledge the better, lest I should be caught between two fires. From the point I had reached the path sloped rapidly and easily down, and I was soon standing on the rock-strewn shore.

And now what was the next thing to be done? Besides the plan of hiding in one of the holes or caverns of the rocks, which was ignominious, and could only delay my discovery for a short time, there was only one other means of escape I could think of; a desperate hazard it was at the best, but desperate diseases require desperate remedies, so I made my preparations to take advantage of the eventuality should it occur.

I did n't exactly know what I had to fear in the event of capture. I could hardly suppose they would deliberately murder me, but I had no wish to try the experiment. The fishermen on that coast are almost a distinct race; they are incredibly savage for a civilized country in this nineteenth century, and like most semi-barbarous people hold human life in very light esteem, except when it is their own that is in question. I had known more than one instance where a man had been kicked or stoned to death in their drunken brawls. By this time they must be thoroughly enraged with me, and what with drink and the excitement of the chase, it was evident that the dogged pertinacity of their characters was roused to the utmost.

About the middle of the cove in which I was standing, there was a reef of rock running out into the sea, one side of which descended abruptly into deep water, while on the other side it shelved gradually, but the bottom was strewn with boulders, so that the point of the reef was the only spot at which it was possible to land from a boat.

To that point I proceeded; having first taken off my coat and boots, and sunk them in the sea, I let myself gently down into the water, and swam carefully along close under the reef, so that no one could see me from above; then I hid myself close to the point, with everything but my head underneath the water, and that covered with seaweed.

Not long afterwards I saw the boat coming round the next headland, and my heart gave a great leap, as I saw fortune had favored me in the first step in that it was a sailing and not a rowing boat that they had brought.

Quickly she neared the point, and half-a-dozen men leapt out, pushing her off again at once and leaving two men in her, evidently to tack about until they returned. Then I dived beneath the water, came up by the stern of the boat, and before she gathered way I had twisted my handkerchief in one of the iron hinges on which the rudder was hung, and clinging to that, was towed through the water, taking care the while to keep the rudder between me and the party on shore. Happily too, it was not one of the whale boats ordinarily used for fishing on the coast that they had got hold of, but an old-fashioned pleasure-boat, half-decked, and with a projecting stern which hid me from the steersman, so that I was safe from his observation as well.

One of the men remarked once that the boat sailed very heavily and the rudder was very stiff, but the other seemed to think that that was only to be expected of such a tub; so nothing further troubled me beyond the smart of the salt water in my cuts, until the boat reached the end of her stretch and tacked; then I let go my hold, and, diving, rose within the shadow of the cliffs out of sight of my enemies, and near a shelving promontory, where I landed.

After that I made the best of my way home, arriving there with no bones broken indeed, but coatless, bootless, gunless, and in such a state of bruises and abrasions as I believe man never was in before. Since then I have gone on no more still-hunting expeditions.

THE NIGHT OF THE HOME RULE BILL

' MISSED again. Here 's better luck. Will you have a nip, Fitzgerald? '

' No, thanks; I never drink when I 'm out shooting. And if I were you, I would n't take any more either. It won't improve your aim.'

' Which is bad enough already. Right you are, my boy. But I admire your cheek in saying so to me, seeing that I 'm twenty years your senior. I suppose I ought to be offended, only I 'm not. But where 's the harm in a flask of whisky in a day? '

' Not the least in life, I suppose, only I 've known good men broken in my time through taking less so early in the day as this. Anyway it does n't make either your hand or your eye any the steadier, and one never knows when he may want all the nerve he 's got.'

The speaker was a District Inspector in the Irish Constabulary, the other was his host, one of that race of gentlemen farmers so fast dying out in Ireland, who had offered him a day on his grouse mountain, the only portion of the estate that was not mortgaged up to the hilt.

'It's about time that I was going home in any case,' continued Fitzgerald.

'Nonsense, man,' cried his companion, 'why, the day is yet young, there'll be light enough to shoot for another two hours, it's hardly four o'clock. What's the hurry?'

'Well, you know that the Home Rule Bill passed its third reading in the House of Commons last night.'

'Yes, and a nice fuss those blackguards are kicking up over it. A mole couldn't help knowing that.'

'That's just it, on the borderland here between Protestantism and Roman Catholicism, the Celtic and Saxon element, party feeling runs extraordinarily high, and the people are so excited that I expect there'll be a row to-night. They're going to have bonfires in the streets and all kinds of games, and we'll be lucky if we get through it without a faction fight. I have to be home and get into uniform before the fun begins, so I hope you don't mind, but I've ordered my man to have the car to meet me at the shebeen by the cross-roads at half-past four.'

'Very well, in that case we'd better be making tracks.   Call the dogs to heel, Jimmie.'

The two men turned and strode down the mountain side, the keeper bringing up the rear with the two pointers.   The heather rustled stiffly against their iron-shod boots as they went, showing behind them a trail of bruised stalks and nail marks on the naked earth. Every now and then, at the sound of their steps a hare rose out of range and dodged swiftly round the corner of a knoll, shrugging her shoulders at the hail-storm of spent shot that rattled round her.   Or a snipe rose with a startling rush and a shrill 'scape, scape' at their feet after being nearly walked over, and zigzagged out of sight.   At the foot of the slope came a belt of rushes with bog-holes gaping for the feet of the unwary.   Beyond that was the first sign of approaching civilization, a potato field, across the ridges of which they strode to reach a cart-track beyond.   A mile along this lay the shebeen they were making for.

'I suppose you'll be very much in evidence

to-night with your men,' remarked Trevor idly, after a time, to break the silence.

' Now, my dear fellow, you might know better than that, after living amongst these people all your life.   There's nothing that provokes an Irishman to make a row so much as to let him know you're ready for him.   Sheer cussedness is a much neglected factor in human nature, and especially Irish nature.   No, of course I have an extra contingent of men in town for the occasion in case of emergency, but my chief endeavor is always to confine them to barracks and to keep them in the background as much as possible.   Their presence only causes friction. More than one of my friends has suffered before now through an undue display of activity.'

' Do you mean that you don't intend to interfere at all, then?'

' Not if I can possibly help it.   If I have to make even one arrest it's all over, it will be a free fight.   The wisdom of those in authority is such, that they have placed the new barracks at the far end of the town from the poorest, and therefore the rowdiest, quarter.   The consequence is that, to run a man in, as a general rule, my men have to drag him about half a mile through the public streets, ánd no Irish mob that was ever raked off its native dung-heap could stand such a temptation as that.'

By this time they had reached the shebeen, a small two-roomed cottage with moss and long grasses growing on its weather-beaten thatched roof. The lower half of the door was shut, but over it they could see the room inside with its hard mud floor; it was furnished with a dresser hung with a few tin porringers and delf plates and bowls, a bedstead and a table; on the hearth was burning a turf fire; in the open chimney-place there swung an iron crook, from which a pot had just been lifted and was now set in the middle of the floor; round it the family, consisting of an old man, a girl and a boy, were gathered upon three-legged stools for their evening meal; each was armed with an iron spoon and a bowl of buttermilk; beside them on some embers a tin teapot was stewing. On the left of the entrance was a half-open door leading into the second room, inside which the sight of some large earthenware crocks of milk and the corner of a bedstead showed that it was used conjointly as a dairy and a sleeping

8

chamber.   Outside the door was the car, with the groom standing at the horse's head.

As the afternoon sun cast their long shadows across the floor of the cottage the old man looked up and saw the two men standing on the doorstep; he rose and opened the half door, and immediately an Irish terrier barking furiously rushed out and attacked the two pointers, that were behind with the keeper.   In a moment the three dogs were rolling together in the road amid a perfect hurricane of yelps.

'Call off your damned mongrel,' shouted Trevor, the veins in his neck purple with rage on behalf of his favorite sporting dogs; but in that rolling mass of liver and white and yellow it was impossible to distinguish one whole animal from another.   'Pull off your dog, Flannigan, or I'll shoot him,' shouted Trevor again, and with his right thumb he pulled up the hammer of his gun, his finger on the trigger.   The old man stooped to separate the dogs; as he did so, Trevor's thumb slipped, the hammer fell, there was a loud report, and the whole charge of shot struck the peasant behind the shoulder at a distance of three yards at most.   He fell with a scream in the middle of the road. The horse stood up on his hind legs pawing at the groom. The dogs rolled into the ditch and continued to worry each other there unnoticed. The rest stood still, stupefied.

'That's what comes of an unsteady hand,' muttered Fitzgerald grimly to himself.

The same instant the girl rushed out of the cottage and threw herself on her father's body. 'Ye've kilt him,' she moaned, 'ye've kilt him.'

At last Trevor recovered himself, and, advancing, laid a hand on her shoulder. 'My good girl,' he said, 'you can't tell how sorry I am that this has occurred. Let us see if we can't help your father. He may not be badly hurt after all.'

'Stan' back,' cried the girl, raising her flushed face and dishevelled hair from the dust and thrusting him violently away. 'Stan' back; don't touch him. Have n't ye done him enough av harrum ahlready?'

'If money's any good,' said Trevor, helplessly making a fresh effort, 'here's all I have with me, and I'll give you — '

'Don't darr to offer me your dirty money,' she interrupted, scattering the coins from his hand with a vehemence of passion that lifted her out of herself. ' It 's blood money, so it is, give me back my father's life that ye tuk away. Did n't I hearn ye say ye 'd shute him, an' shute him ye did, an' may the curse of the fatherless rist on ye from this day out.'

' Nonsense, girl,' said Fitzgerald hastily, ' it was a pure accident, and Mr. Trevor never threatened to shoot your father, but only the dog, and the gun went off by accident in his hand.'

' An accident was it? An accident? ' repeated the girl. ' An' arn't yous a polisman and you stood by and seen it done? Why don't ye arrist him? I 'll larn ye if it was an accident or not,' and she stooped down and whispered some words in her brother's ear, her eyes gleaming with all the fierce vindictiveness of the Celtic nature when roused. The boy nodded silently and darted quickly off down the road, looking back from time to time; Fitzgerald gazed uneasily after him for a moment, then turning briskly to the keeper, he said, ' Hurry up to the house and tell Mrs. Trevor to send down some brandy and some linen for bandages. And you, Jackson, run across the fields to Doherty's there behind the hill. The doctor 's there now, so bring him back with you. And you,' he continued, laying his hand on the girl's arm, ' must let us carry your father in out of this. He can't be left here any longer or he 'll bleed to death.'

The girl stood sullenly on one side while the two men unhinged the door, placed the old man upon it as carefully as possible, carried him in and laid him on the bed. Then Fitz-gerald cut the clothes away from the gaping wound, tore up one of the coarse sheets, and bound the injured part up roughly but not unskilfully. The fowls ran in and out of the open door the while and pecked unnoticed at the pot of potatoes upon the floor.

' I think we 've done everything that can be done now,' said the D. I. when he had finished, ' and there 's no good stopping here. It 's time that I was in town, and the doctor 'll be round here immediately. I 'll send the priest up to you as soon as I get there. I 'm afraid I must trouble you, Trevor, to come with me.'

' Why? What 's the meaning of this?' stam-mered the farmer, his face going ashen gray.

' I 'm afraid that after what 's happened,' answered Fitzgerald formally, looking intently at the ground, and digging a root of grass out of the roadway with his toe, ' that it is my duty not to let you out of my sight.'

' Ha!' ejaculated the girl, her nostrils dilating, and a succession of strange emotions, satisfaction, doubt and anxiety, chasing each other rapidly across her expressive features.

The disgraced man walked towards the car and clambered up on one side like a man in a dream, his companion mounted the other and drove rapidly away. As soon as they were out of earshot of the girl, he said, ' the fact is, that in the present excited state of feeling in the country, you are much safer for a few nights in our barracks than in your own house.' Trevor said nothing. These words explained his companion's attitude, but it did not affect the sudden realization of the outer consequences of his act, which had come upon him like a blow. His senses were stunned for the time being, and only perceived an endless vista of stone walls swiftly hurrying past.

Rounding the first corner, out of sight of the cottage, the D. I. urged his horse to a gallop, which he kept up the whole six miles to the town. The road consisted of a succession of steep hills joining plateau to plateau, and lead-

ing always downwards from the higher ground
to the valley beneath. Down these the light
car rattled and bounced, jolting and swaying
as either wheel passed over a larger fragment
of rock than usual; often for yards at a time
their velocity carried them along upon one
wheel, the other spinning violently in the air;
the smaller stones flew to every side from the
good gray horse's hoof-strokes as he stretched
to his work over the flint-strewn road. Soon
the poor beast was in a lather, but neither of
the men moved or spoke or took note of the
rush fields, with the sod walls between, that
flitted past, each one so like the last that they
appeared to get not a step further on their
journey. It was a nightmare of endless same-
ness. Still they sat fast, the one straining his
eyes eagerly over the winding road beneath
them, the other looking straight in front of
him with eyes that saw nothing and a mind
that had no room for wonder at such furious
haste upon the part of a man who was proverbially merciful to his cattle.

As they approached the town, Fitzgerald's
face grew longer and longer, and he drove ever
more and more recklessly, until they had

clattered and slithered down the last hill, and sweeping round the curve, came in sight of a figure running laboriously along the dusty road in front of them.   Then his eyes lightened, and he muttered to himself: 'I think we can just do it; but it was a narrow squeak, I allowed him too long a start on such a hilly road.'   The figure, when they overtook it, proved to be that of the wounded man's son; the blood was streaming from gashes in his naked feet, where they had been cut by the sharp flints upon the rough mountain road, and his breath was coming in deep sobs.   As the car drew abreast of him, he caught hold of the step beneath Trevor's feet and ran by his side for a few paces, but the driver leaned across the well of the car and slashed at him savagely with the whip; the long, thin lash lapped itself round the ragged body and bare legs of the lad, nearly spinning him off his feet as it uncurled.   He let go his hold with a yell of pain, and dropped behind showing his teeth in a grin of disappointed malevolence; but still he continued doggedly running on.

'That was Flannigan's son, surely,' said Trevor, startled out of his trance.

'I know,' replied Fitzgerald briefly, whipping up his horse afresh, and soon the boy was hidden from them in a rolling cloud of dust. But on turning the next corner they found themselves at the beginning of the long street of the little town, and he had to slacken pace again. The roadway was blocked with heaps of wood and tar-barrels, and behind each pane of glass in the wretched windows the length of the street was fixed a tallow candle, in readiness for the illumination of the evening. Groups of men were lounging about the doorways, amongst whom were seen a few women wearing white aprons, the badge of 'the most ancient profession in the world.'

The car threaded its way with difficulty through these varied obstructions, the police officer and his friend being the recipients of more than one scowling glance or smothered curse; but once clear of them, Fitzgerald urged the horse to his speed again, and galloped up the hill beyond.

'What's all the hurry about?' asked Trevor, now awake to his surroundings.

'That boy is here to tell them about you,' was the reply; and he relapsed into silence

again, his position brought home to him more
forcibly than ever.

The next moment a shout was heard, followed by a hoarse roar; and looking down the
slope they could see, in the gathering dusk, a
black mass surging up the hill behind them,
the white aprons gleaming in the forefront
like the feathering of surf upon a wind-blown
billow. But the barrack gates had clanged to
behind them before the foremost of their pursuers could come within reach, and the mob
swept in a torrent round the base of the building, uttering cries of rage, and leaping up
against the walls, like wolves who have been
disappointed of their prey.

'Give him up to us,' they shouted. 'We want
the murdherer of Pether Flannigan.   We 'll
tear the heart out of the bloody tyrant.'

'The black curse be on the quality,' screamed
a woman's strident treble, high above the rest.
'Give us the man that 's made orphans of a
poor man's childer, or we 'll pull the whole
place about yer ears.'

'Faith,' said Fitzgerald with a gentle chuckle,
'that was a near thing; and, all things considered, I 'm just as well pleased after all that

the barracks are not in the middle of their quarter to-night, or there 's no knowing what might happen.'

The whole of that night all kinds of rumors were rife in the town, but nothing definite was ascertained. Orators declaimed to excited crowds round the bonfires, rousing them to boiling-point. The Catholics, especially those of the baser sort, were loud in their accusations against Trevor, denouncing the accident as a deliberate cold-blooded murder, and finding in it a political significance as the last act of despairing tyranny on the part of the Saxon in revenge for his overthrow. They swore that the man who had thus dared to insult the hopes of a budding nation should pay for his insolent mockery with his blood. The other party shrugged their shoulders, and declared it would be folly to interfere with the Nationalists in such a mood; it was hard lines on Trevor, no doubt, but it was his own fault for being such a fool. If he were once returned for trial, it would be all up with him; for no Irish jury would be found to acquit him, and the Government would not dare to interfere at such a crisis. The only hope for him was that the man should not die at all, and that could hardly be called a hope.

The next morning, hearing that Flannigan had taken a turn for the worse, Fitzgerald set out with a magistrate, in order to take his deposition before the end should come. Half-way there they met the doctor returning from his visit. He told them that the charge of shot had completely shattered the shoulder-blade — a wound which was not necessarily mortal in the case of a young man of strong constitution; but at his patient's age, the shock to the system alone was bound to prove fatal, and he was rapidly sinking, though he had still some hours of life before him. As he was leaving, the priest had actually arrived to administer the last offices to the dying man.

'I think,' said Fitzgerald, as the doctor drove on upon his way, 'that I'll walk up one or two of these hills. This poor beast of mine got rather a gruelling last night, and I don't want him to have a permanent grudge against this road;' and, to the magistrate's surprise, he walked the whole of the remainder of the journey.

As they came up to the cottage, they could see, as once before, over the half door into its interior. The priest was standing by the bedside holding the vessel of holy oil in his hands; and through the crisp morning air the last words of the sacrament of Extreme Unction rang clear upon their ears:

'Through this holy unction,' and they could see the sweep of the priest's arm, as he made the sign of the cross upon the sick man's forehead, 'and through His most tender mercy the Lord pardon thee whatever sins thou hast committed with the senses of thy body and with the thoughts and desires of thy heart. Amen.'

'Amen,' echoed the two men, and swinging open the half door entered the room. The priest turned from bestowing the blessing, and his eyes fell upon the magistrate; he started, and a sudden flame of apprehension leapt into life in his eyes, which was answered by a smile deep down in Fitzgerald's. And then was seen a curious sight: a conflict of religions, of parties, of races, over the dying body of one man. Another human life was the stake.

'I have come to take your deposition,' said the magistrate, advancing into the room to the side of the bed.

'Why, how is this?' interrupted the priest hoarsely, licking his lips with his tongue. 'Why was I not told that this had not been done?'

'Why, what differ does it make?' asked the girl anxiously from the foot of the bed.

The priest's nostrils distended and he opened his mouth to speak, but restrained himself. He turned to the bed and said: 'You wish to depose that Mr. Trevor shot you after having threatened to do so?'

'Ay,' said the man; 'he said he 'd shute me, an' shute me he did.'

Anxiety gave way to triumph in the priest's eyes, but prematurely, for the dying man's gaze followed Fitzgerald's significant look to the sacred vessel that the priest still grasped in his hand, and he continued — 'But what is all that to me? I 'm done with the affairs of this life. I 've had my absolution for all my sins thought and done. I 'm done with the wurruld an' the wurruld 's done with me. I 'm nat to ate nor spake more. An' I forgive him.'

'You need n't mind about the absolution,' urged the priest in his eagerness, letting the mask slip, and the glare of fanaticism shine through, 'I 'll see that that 's made all right:

I 'll get you a dispensation. But you must
make some statement before you die.'

'I tell ye,' said the old man querulously, and
raising himself excitedly upon his elbow, 'I
forgive him. Foreby, Misther Trevor's bin a
good master to me up to now. An' I 'll make
no statement. An' I won't be stirred from that
wurrud by man nor praste.' But the effort was
too much for him, and the next moment he fell
back upon the pillow gasping, the bed dyed red
with his life-blood; his wound had broken out
afresh.

With a despairing cry his daughter threw
herself on her knees by the bedside, and the
two laymen unbaring themselves reverently in
the presence of Death, withdrew into the open
air to await his advent. Ten minutes afterwards the old man had ceased to breathe,
without having again opened his lips.

'It 's lucky for our friend Trevor,' said Fitzgerald to his companion, as they drove thoughtfully homeward, 'that the priest made that
mistake about the sacrament, and that the
Irish peasant has such an ingrained reverence
for forms. The old man was evidently set
upon his delusion, whether he got it from his

daughter or no, and if he had made that statement, you would have had to commit Trevor
for trial, and he would equally surely have
been hanged.   As it is, I don't think any com-
mittal is necessary.'

'Now I know why you were so anxious to
walk up all those hills,' the magistrate dryly
replied; 'but it would n't have done to arrive
after his death.'

'No; that would n't have done at all. The
fat would have been in the fire then, with a
vengeance.   But, as it is, they have no cause
for complaint.'

It turned out as Fitzgerald said.   When the
case was brought before them for a preliminary
hearing, the magistrates decided that in the
face of his victim's refusal to testify against
Trevor there was no case for a jury.   At this
decision there was agitation in some quarters,
and talk about class feeling and the straining
of justice on behalf of individuals; but everybody felt that both sides were tarred with the
same brush, and the Catholics no doubt perceived that they had sold themselves: the
better sort amongst them sympathized with
Trevor's misfortune, and held aloof from the

more extreme element. The matter was not vigorously pushed, and soon dropped into oblivion.

But the incident left its permanent mark upon Trevor. He was too soft-fibred to pass through such a fiery ordeal unscathed. Added to the fact of having a fellow-creature's life upon his hands, a man of his inoffensive type could not feel a whole community thirsting for his blood and show no sign thereafter. From that day he retired completely into himself, holding aloof from his neighbors, and within a few months had grown old and broken down before his time.

A BORDER WAR

'For God's sake give me a drink of whisky and soda to wash my heart down; it's been in my mouth all day,' said Fitzgerald, clattering into the room in his war panoply, his sword clanking against his spurs, and throwing himself into my favorite easy chair.

'What's the matter?' I asked, as I filled him a three-finger drink and put the decanter and siphon beside him.

'What! Have n't you heard the news, you benighted heathen? Why, the whole country's ringing with it.'

'Cease to praise your own exploits, and trot out your story,' I said firmly, 'or I'll take away the whisky.'

'Well,' he began, after draining his glass at a draught, 'from information received, as they say in the force, I learnt yesterday that there had been the beginnings of a pretty little fight

up in the near end of Robertson's district.
And I knew that he was due at the Assizes at
the other end of the County to-day, so I
thought I 'd keep my eye on the case for him.

'It seems that up in that part there is a spot
where the two counties meet and also the
boundaries of two large properties. By a
mistake in the survey at some time a strip of
field just there was omitted: the county line
runs down the middle of it, but it is claimed by
neither of the landowners. It is mere rushy
land, not worth ten shillings an acre, and of no
account to a rich man, but to the half-starved
peasant of these parts even that much grass is
a perfect treasure-trove.

'Under these circumstances the tenants of
the two nearest cabins on either side of the
field have been accustomed by tacit agreement
to look upon· this strip as their own property.
Each took the county line as the boundary or
marin of his claim, and each mowed his own
half. But the one that came first generally
encroached a little, and stole as much of his
neighbor's grass as he thought he could with
safety. Of recent years this habit had increased,
and led to considerable jealousy between the

two men; and as the land belonged to nobody
except by prescriptive right, it became more or
less of a public question in the district, and the
men of each county espoused the cause of their
respective champions.

'Well, yesterday morning, as luck would
have it, both men took it into their heads to
mow their piece on the same day, and both
arrived on the ground together. They eyed
each other suspiciously: then they started
mowing at the two extremities opposite each
other and began to race for the middle of the
field, each determined to see that the other did
not trespass on his portion.

'The faster mower arrived first, and in his
haste appropriated a scytheful of his neighbor's grass, which was easy to do, as nothing
but an imaginary line divided the two halves
of the field.

'Directly afterwards the other man came
opposite him and saw what had occurred, and
a black scowl gathered upon his face. He
stooped down and picked up a stone against
which his scythe-blade had just rasped: he
spat on it and put it carefully upon the middle
of the imaginary line, then he said:

' "That's the marin, Larry Scanlan, and that's my mark. Stir a fut acrost it agin, if ye darr, an' I'll stretch ye as dacint a corp as ever ye seen."

'"Ah," replied the other, roused by this insult, "give me any more ov yer lip, Con Doherty, an I'll jist dhraw me han' an' hit yous a skelp that ull knock ye endways from here to Ameriky."

' They glared fiercely at each other, and having thus crowed their mutual defiance, there seemed nothing left to do but to fight.

' But each looked at the scythe in the hands of the other, and hesitated to begin the fray. The ideal scythe-blade is not smooth and sharp: such would soon lose its edge and be a cause of bad language to its owner. But the scythe that delights the mower's heart has a ripple like the teeth of a saw ground down, that grips the grass-stalks and shears straight through them. A heavy blade like this would drive through cloth and flesh and bone, and lop off limbs as a pruning-knife lops twigs. It is a formidable weapon in a row. Each man pondered the unknown quantity of how far his neighbor would be prepared to go if his blood were up. Meanwhile the situation lagged.

' Doherty was the smaller man and already regretted his rash procedure. As he gazed round to the earth and sky for inspiration his eye lit upon his brother digging potatoes in the adjoining field, and thoughts of reinforcements came to him.

' " Come over here a minute, Roger," he shouted, " I want ye."

' Roger came with his spade. And a neighbor that was passing by sat upon the wall to watch the fight.

' " Now," said Con triumphantly, "quit the groun', or we 'll scarify ye."

' But Scanlan scented an opportunity to base his private quarrel on the grounds of public principle, and said to the neighbor, who fortunately lived on the same side of the marin as himself :

' " Shure now, Pather, ye wud n't stan' by an say a man av yer own county putt upon by them dhirty land-grabbin' furriners."

' Peter looked at the group and saw that Larry was the biggest of the three. He was not above having "a bit ov fun," so long as he was likely to be on the winning side. He had his spade with him also. So he spat on his

hands, grasped the handle, and ranged himself
on the side of his county, saying briefly;

'"I'll stan' by ye, Larry."

'So once more the situation had arrived at a
deadlock. The advantage lay with neither side.
But the delay had allowed the blood of the two
original combatants to cool, and their thoughts
turned upon strategy.   After a few more
mutual recriminations they separated by tacit
consent, and each went his way, muttering
darkly to himself:

'"Wait till the morra, an' we'll see what yous
ull luke like thin."

'But when two men hit upon a plan, whose
methods of life and grooves of thought have
been the same from their birth upward, it is
likely that the ideas of both will be very
similar.   So that night the fiery cross, as it were,
ran through the surrounding district on both
sides of the border . . . This morning at the
hush of dawn a murmur arose on each side of
the field in dispute.   And the sun shed its first
rays upon a hundred men sitting upon the stone
ditch on one side of the field, and a hundred
upon the other.   Each side gazed in blank
surprise to find its idea anticipated.   And all

through the forenoon men came dropping in by
twos and threes, armed with their scythes, to
reinforce their own party and reap the grass
for their county.

'About twelve o'clock two boys came to me
within a few minutes of each other with a
message to "Come up to Doherty's marin at
wanst, or there'll be could murther done."

'I thought two messengers argued great
urgency, and set off in hot haste with my four-
and-twenty policemen.   When we arrived upon
the ground we found a full couple of thousand
men sitting on each ditch facing each other.
I drew up my forces in the middle of the field
between them, facing both ways, felt like
Leonidas, and wished myself somewhere else.

'But neither party took the slightest notice
of our presence.   They sat on their respective
walls and went on shouting their challenges
across our heads as though we did not exist.
One man would shout:

' "Ah, come over here, Tim Daly, an' I'll put
a face on ye that yer own mother wud n't know
ye."

'And the other side would reply:

' "Wait till I come te you, ye yelpin' cub, an'

I 'll stritch yer mouth both ways roun' yer head."

'Both parties waited and nothing occurred.

'At last the situation began to dawn upon me. Neither of them cared a damn for me and my policemen, but each faction had too healthy a respect for the strength of the other to take the first step. And then the meaning of the two messengers also became plain — one had been despatched by either side at the same time both desiring an honorable retreat from the difficult position into which they had got themselves. For nowadays even Irishmen are not used to a faction fight in which the combatants upon either side number two thousand strong and are armed with scythes. The situation was too big for their stomachs, and each man said to himself, as he gazed upon the black mass gathered at the other side of the field, "This job is a bit too thick. I wish I was safe at home."

'Now a novice, as soon as he discovered the position of affairs, would have thought everything quite safe, and would consequently have made a mess of it. But I know these people thoroughly: I have lived — '

'Cut the cackle,' I said, 'and continue the story.   We 'll take all your perfections as read.'

'Well, as I was saying, when you interrupted me so rudely, I knew that because I had fathomed the situation we were not necessarily safe out of it.   If but a spark were added to their combativeness, we were in for the biggest fight that I had seen in my time, and between the two we police would be the first to suffer.

'So I walked warily.   I waited until one of the men came to a well near us for a drink of water.   Then I called him, and after several other questions about the condition of affairs, I asked him the name of the leader upon the other side.

'Directly he had gone back to his fellows, I walked towards the opposite crowd and asked for Larry Scanlan.

'He came out to meet me, and I said to him,

'"I 've done my best, but Doherty's men are simply raging for a fight, and I can't keep them in hand a minute longer.   For God's sake, draw off your party, or I won't answer for the consequences: they 'll eat you up body and bones."

'The man went a grayish green, shaking

with terror, and said, "For the luv of Mary, sir, don't let us be murthered. What will we do at ahl?"

'Then I said that if they were out of sight of their opponents my task would be easier: if they withdrew in a body to the next ditch when I waved my handkerchief I would reason with Doherty's men, and would be able to bring him their proposals for an agreement.

'Scanlan consented, and I went over to the opposite side, drew an equally terrifying picture of the bloodthirsty eagerness of their adversaries, and made the same arrangement.

'Then I returned to my devoted corps, waved my handkerchief, and Hey, Presto! not a man was to be seen anywhere.

'I waited patiently for five minutes, and then sent a couple of my men to reconnoitre. They returned and reported that when they arrived at the second ditch in each direction not a figure was to be seen on the whole countryside. As soon as they had got out of sight of the enemy both armies had fled swiftly, every man to his own home.

'Well, I was n't going to leave the occasion of offence behind me, so I drew a line down the centre of the field from marin stone to marin stone, sent into the surrounding parts and hired a dozen mowers, and in three hours I had that field mown and the grass gathered upon either hand with a space of twelve yards between; and if they like to go back and fight over it now, they can fight: for I'm not going to interfere again. I've had enough of them.'

'And what are you going to get out of all this heroism and astuteness?' I asked.

'I? Oh if it ever comes to the ears of the authorities, I shall get a slating for interfering outside my own district, and I consider I richly deserve it. As it is I have already got out of it a beautiful thirst, that I wouldn't sell for half-a-crown. Give us another drink, old man.'

'And how much of that story is true?' I asked, 'and how much is your tropical imagination?'

'That,' said he, 'is for you to decide, my boy,' and he deliberately winked his left eye at me.

A NIGHTMARE CLIMB

'No, I like you very much, but there can never be anything of that kind between us.'

'I expected this. But I think you are very foolish,' replied the young man slowly, twisting his moustache.

The girl was too astonished at this superior way of taking a rejection to say anything. It was beyond her experience entirely.

'Of course,' he continued, 'Elsie — Miss Derwent, I have seen that you do not love me as I love you. I have only opened the subject to set my case before you. You know me very well, and you say that you like me. You are quite aware that I have been in love with you for the last five years, though I have not spoken until I had a position to offer you. That position I have made for myself. You were my guiding star. All the hours that I have labored, till my work tasted bitter in my mouth, it was for the hope of you I persevered. And now I am not to be lightly cheated of my reward. It is best that most of the love should be on the man's side, and I am content to wait for your love till after marriage. I know that I can win it. You are a woman and no longer a girl, so you should be above romantic notions on the subject.'

She flushed, and he saw immediately that he had made a false move. By those last few words he had lost all the ground that he had won. So he began over again.

'You know my family, too, and like them. And you must see, though I say it, who should n't, that my two sisters idolize me. The man who makes a good brother or son is likely to make a good husband. I would make you a good husband, the best you are ever likely to get. You will never find any one who will understand you so thoroughly as I do after all these years, any one with so many tastes in common, or who will love you so entirely for your real self, and not for any impossible ideal of woman-hood you may represent to the imagination.'

'You can blow your own trumpet well, at any rate,' she said with a smile.

' Why not? If I don't blow it myself nobody else is likely to do so for me. Shakespeare says something somewhere to the effect that a man is a poor creature who can't persuade a woman to love him. I think it runs :

> " That man that hath a tongue, I say is no man,
> If with his tongue he cannot win a woman."

And I quite agree with him. I am not going to risk my life's happiness now for the sake of a few scruples of delicacy. I am no braggart. Ask any of my men friends, and they will tell you, that they have never known me to boast. But I will boast now — I am not a coward, and I tell you I would lay down my life for your sake. I only wish the occasion might occur, that I might prove my words. '

' The occasion never does occur nowadays. The age of knight-errantry is past. And in any case it is a very poor thing to do. To die only requires a moment's resolution after all. What we women want is, not a man who will die for us, but one who will live for us. '

' Well, there too I am ready to fulfil your wants. You have lived for the last month in the same house with me, and tell me if I have ever been anything but charming. The man whose temper can stand the ordeal of continual companionship for a month in a country-house in this God-forsaken place, can stand anything. Therefore marry me. Is not that common-sense?'

'Yes,' she said with a little spite, feeling that she was illogical. 'That is just what I object to. You are so sensible, so horridly, vulgarly successful, self-confident, good-natured, and altogether admirable. You are too perfect. If I ought not to admire you so much, I might perhaps — like you more.'

'You are frank at any rate,' said he ruefully.

'Yes. It will do you good to hear for once in a way, that you are too conceited and philosophical. You have too much common-sense. What business has a lover to talk common-sense, I should like to know. Any one can do that. However it is useless to argue any further, Mr. Travers. My mind is made up. I will never marry a man I do not love. And I do not — care for you, as you would have me.'

'But will you not try and love me?'

'Love does not come by trying,' quoth the maiden sententiously.

'Nevertheless I will not despair. But meanwhile I hope you will not let this interfere with our arrangements for this last day, or with your stay here. I cannot get a telegram summoning me on urgent business till the morning. But I will go then. This afternoon you know you promised to come on an expedition to see our Donegal cliffs, and the Pigeons' Cave especially; while I am to get you those cormorant's eggs you wished for.'

'Very well, I will go.'

At the appointed time they set out on an Irish car. In the well Travers, who was driving, took a stake with a pulley at the end and a coil of rope, a relic of his boyhood's days, when he used to be great at bird's-nesting. The party consisted to all intents and purposes of himself and Miss Derwent. The other three, two men and a girl, were mere nonentities, who had been invited as make-weights. Travers, with still unsubdued pride of intellect, had christened them in his own mind as the Fool, the Idiot, and the Inane Girl.

When they arrived at Kilcross, the other four went down a winding path on the side of the cliff, and proceeded along the shore in the direction of the Pigeons' Cave. Travers

went across the headlands to the same spot,
and fixed his stake in the turf above some
crevices in the rock, where he knew of old he
would find the cormorant's eggs he was in
search of.   He would first join the rest of the
party, he thought, in their sight-seeing.   Afterwards they would all come up to the top and
lower him down in search of his prey.

By the time he had finished arranging the
stake, the others were underneath him.   So he
shouted to them he would come the shortest
way down.   Lowering the rope until the bight
at the end touched the rocks below, he fastened
the upper end by twisting it a couple of times
round the stake, and thrusting the slack carelessly, as he afterwards remembered, under the
part of the rope between the top round and the
pulley.   There would only be a very slight strain
for a few moments in sliding down, and he had
often before descended a rope fastened like that.

He lowered himself gently over the edge of
the cliff, and this time, as usual, slid safely
down, landing at the feet of the four below.

'How quickly you came down, Mr. Travers,'
simpered the Inane Girl.

'Oh! I'm used to climbing, and it comes as

naturally to me as sliding down the banisters did to you, when you were a small girl.'

' I never slid down banisters,' she replied austerely.

' The Queen of Spain has no legs,' quoted Travers to himself.

Then they went on to the Pigeons' Cave, which was close at hand. As they reached the entrance, Travers said:

' Take cate you don't fall into that pool, ladies, this green seaweed is very slippery.'

Once inside they found themselves in a huge rock cavern of a hard yellow stone, which was formed by petrifaction, and which was still in process of growth around them. The sides were covered with moisture which was gradually turning into stone. From the roof depended clusters of giant stalactites, formed by the ceaseless drip of ages, giving the cave the appearance of the fretted aisles of some huge cathedral. From these festooned arches there flew forth at the clapping of their hands a blue cloud of rock-pigeons, flitting like shadows, or like ' squealing bats,' in the dusky twilight of the cavern, till for a moment they obscured the daylight at the entrance. These made their nests in the lofty roof, and gave the cave its name.

Travers, laughing, regretted he could not get some of their eggs too. But that could not be done by any means short of bringing a fire-escape upon the scene.

'But come along to the inner end of the cave, girls, and I'll give you a drink from the Wishing Well,' he said. 'As its name implies, it has power to ensure you anything you may desire as you drink its waters, from your lover's fidelity to the quenching of your thirst.'

So saying he got the other two men to hoist him up to a ledge which he could just reach with his hands; then drawing himself up onto it, he filled the silver cup of his flask from a recess at the back, and handed it down to the ladies.

'It's very nice and cool,' said the Inane Girl, 'but how does it come up there?'

'I believe it is merely the drippings from the rock collected in a small hollow. It is to be hoped it won't petrify inside you.'

'Oh! yes,' said she, 'I hear it dripping, now you mention it. Why, it's trickling quite fast.'

'Trickling! Good heavens! We must get out of this at once. Quick! Help me down.'

'Why, what's the matter? Anything wrong?' they all chorussed.

' Yes, everything. That trickling is the tide coming into the pool at the mouth of the cave, and it will soon be too late for us to escape, if it is not already.'

When they reached the mouth of the cave, one glance was sufficient. The breakers were already beating against the rocks at the extremity of either horn of the bay. No one would round those corners until the next tide.

The others wished to run and see if escape was hopeless. But Travers prevented them. It would only be waste of time and energy.

' Then I suppose we must just wait in the cave till the tide goes down again,' said Miss Derwent, while the Inane Girl bleated, ' Oh! we 'll all be drowned, I 'm sure we will.'

' No,' said Travers sternly; ' we cannot remain in the cave. The tide washes right up to the end of it. I have got you into this scrape, and I 'm bound to get you out of it.' He spoke to the other girl but he looked at Miss Derwent.

' The ledge,' he continued, ' where the Wishing Well is situated is above high-water mark, but I doubt whether you could get up to it, and in

any case it would only hold one.   Then it is a
mile and a half to swim round those rocks to
any landing-place, and by the time I could
return with a boat, you would be past praying
for.   No!   I see nothing for it but the rope.'

'The rope?   What do you mean?'

'The rope here that I came down by.   I will
climb up it, and then haul you up after me one
by one.   Fortunately it swings clear of the cliff
the whole way up.'

'Isn't it very dangerous?' said the Inane
Girl.

'Oh! not at all.   It's only a hundred feet or
so.   I'm used to gymnastics, and have always
been fond of climbing.   So it will be all right.'

'Oh! I wasn't thinking of you,' she replied.
'I was thinking I shouldn't like to be pulled up
all that way by a rope.'

'You'll be lucky if you get the chance,'
growled Travers grimly to himself.   'And now
girls, I must trouble you to go into the cave
again for a minute, as I have to take off some
of my clothes.   Keep them there as long as
you can', he whispered to one of the men.
'I don't want to have them underneath when
I'm going up.'

'Do you think you can do it?' said the other man, who remained behind with him.

'I'm sure I don't know. It's a good two hundred feet, and I have never done so much before. Then this rope is very thin for climbing. But what troubles me most — but there, it's no good talking about it. I must do it. Say good-bye to them for me if I don't come back — or rather, if I do, as I suppose you can hardly spread a blanket to catch me by yourself. In that case the only thing to do is to go back into the cave as far as possible, and pray that it may not be a high tide.'

He stripped to his knickerbockers and stockings, for every ounce would tell against him in the struggle before him, tied a handkerchief round his waist and began the ascent slowly, hand over hand, the muscles standing out like cords on his uncovered arms and chest.

When half the distance was done, he stopped for a rest. Half the remainder, and once again he paused. Soon after the terrible doubt, that he had hinted at, recurred to his mind with fresh force. He was not progressing as fast as he ought. The rope must be slipping off the stake. He stopped again, and watched the

cliff opposite him.   No, it was only his imagination.   He was quite steady.   The last few
yards were a terrible struggle, but he managed
them somehow, and, reaching the top, dropped
upon the turf, his head swimming, his limbs
trembling, and his muscles twitching with the
prolonged tension they had undergone.

After a time he rose and went to the stake,
when he received a shock which made him feel
sick and faint with fear, unnerving him even
more than his climb itself.   A cold sweat broke
out all over him.   His throat grew dry and
parched, and a scum gathered on his lips and
the roof of his mouth.   When he tied the rope
originally there were several yards over.   Now
there was only a single foot left protruding.
As he had thought at the time, the rope had
been gradually unreeling itself from the stake,
all the while he was ascending.   When he
remained still, the steady strain did not affect
it.   But the post being of polished wood, the
movement he made in climbing caused the
rope to slip round its smooth surface in jerks.
Another dozen jerks and he would have been
dashed to pieces on the rocks below.

He nearly fainted at the thought.   But the

recollection of those below came to him and revived him. He could not afford to give way just yet. But when he had hauled one of the other men up and asked him to do the same by the rest, he lay down again on the grass, and when Miss Derwent came up, she found that the strong man had swooned away.

When Travers regained consciousness his head was lying on her lap, and she was forcing some brandy between his teeth.

' You are safe, then,' he said, ' so I did not fall after all.'

When he had dressed himself they all went back to the car. But Travers said he was too unnerved to drive, and asked the Idiot, though he called him so no longer even in his own mind, to take the reins and his seat in the middle. The other man and the girl had already taken their places on one side. So that left the remaining side to him and Miss Derwent.

She will never forget that drive to her dying day.

She had him practically to herself, for the others' backs were all turned upon them. For a good opportunity for love-making commend me to an Irish outside car. It is solitude in the midst of a crowd.

But they were not thinking of love-making now. At first Travers made a few disjointed remarks, but gradually he became silent. She saw the white dazed look stealing over his face, which she had first noticed at the top of the cliff. He began muttering to himself. Then suddenly he burst out:—

'That's half-way, only a hundred feet more.' It was evident that he was living over again that terrible climb of his. But this time he was conscious of his danger. She listened spellbound.

'I wonder if I can last it out. I must. Those rocks looked very hard. Fifty feet more. My God! The rope is slipping. No, it is only my imagination. The cliff opposite me is quite still. Twenty feet more. I must pass that tuft of grass. I didn't reach it as quick as I ought. The rope *is* slipping. Every jerk brings me nearer to destruction It is cutting into my hands. My arms are coming out of their sockets. My legs are numbed. I must let go. Only two yards more. For her sake! I wonder if she is watching me. I must look down and see. Oh! it has come away in my hand. I am falling, falling through the air. There is nothing to catch hold of. G—r—r—r! Keep her away, you fool. Why did you let her see such a mess as that?'

As in a nightmare she listened to the slow progress of that horrible struggle. The sentences were jerked one by one from his tongue, as from the tongue of the mesmerized dead man in Poe's terrible story. There was a pause between each. He drew his breath in gasps, as though in mortal conflict. His face became more and more drawn and ghastly, and drooped till it was completely hidden from her sight. His body grew limp. At every jolt of the car it sagged further downwards, as though about to dive into the road at their feet.

Terrified, she shook him, screamed 'Percy' in his ear; but he did not hear. Then in desperation she softly nipped the fleshy part of his arm. The pain brought him to himself. He sat bolt upright with a start, like one that has been nodding, and is suddenly awakened.

'Have I been saying anything?' he inquired, anxiously.

'Ah! I am glad. I thought perhaps I might have been talking nonsense.' They did not speak again for the remainder of the drive. The others had noticed nothing, — all their attention was taken up with the perennial Irish rain, which was driving in their faces.

The next morning he was ill, and unable to leave his room. But when they met in the afternoon, he said with a wan smile, 'I am sorry to have broken my promise. And I am afraid I must ask you to excuse my presence here this evening as well. I have lost my nerve. I daren't travel in a train. I am afraid.' He made the confession with a burst, as though it were wrung from him.

'If you like, I will go away instead,' she replied slowly, drooping her head.

'No, please don't,' he said imploringly. 'I feel safer when you are near me.'

The boyish pathos and abandonment of his tone joined to his utter weakness and prostration did for him what his previous confident strength, and even the fact of his having risked his life for hers, had failed to effect. Her experience of the day before upon the car had shown her what he had gone through to thus jangle his nerves. It was in her service this stroke had come upon him. She could not blame him for it, nor to her could it bear the aspect of cowardice. For no woman can forgive that. Her woman's heart was melted. The requisite touch of tenderness was added to her feeling for him. The tears gushed to her eyes.

'You know I said yesterday, you were too perfect,' she murmured.

'Yes, well?'

'I don't think you so perfect now.'

'My darling.'

They kissed each other passionately.

Under her care Travers' nerves soon recovered their normal tone. But since that day he has never boasted again of his courage. His wife says, that the next lover she has shall be philosophical too. For that kind make the best husbands after all.

A PEASANT TRAGEDY

PART I

THE LOVERS

A GROUP of peasants were straggling along the hilly road returning from the fair in the summer twilight. It was composed of about an equal number of men and women; the women trudged along on their naked feet, with their heavy market-baskets over one arm, and their boots slung by the laces over the other; the men lazily dragged their heavily shod feet after them, with the trailing gait born of much walking in ploughed fields and clinging soil, they carried one hand in their trousers' pocket, the other twirling an ash plant, with which they switched off the heads of all the thistles they met.

In front of them wandered a few young bullocks, badly bred and unkempt, mooing pitifully from time to time. In their midst was a donkey-cart with four sheep and a couple of pigs confined between its cribs; the sheep were tied together in pairs with twisted hay-bands round their necks, their legs also were hobbled with hay-bands; the pigs ran about loose and routed ceaselessly among the straw at the bottom of the cart. The donkey plodded patiently along by himself, for the most part unnoticed; but when it was necessary to turn aside into a by-road or avoid one of the huge stones that had tumbled off a neighboring ditch, one of the men guided him by the simple but effective means of seizing the tail-pieces and levering round both cart and staggering donkey together.

'A bad fair agin the day,' said one of the elder men in a high querulous tone, directed impartially to the group at large.

'Ay, deed so,' replied another, 'times is main bad the now. Bastes is gone clane to nothin'; two pun I was bid the day for a year-ould heifer; that's her runnin' in front wi' the white patch 'roun' her tail; I min' the time when I would n't have luked at sivin for her; two pun, min' that now,' and he spat disgustedly. 'Pigs is the on'y thing as fetches any price at ahl, an' who's to be at the cost of fattenin' thim?'

' Michael Dolan wud n't be overly well plazed at yon sight,' interjected the first speaker, jerking his thumb over his shoulder in the direction of the hindmost of the group.

The couple thus alluded to were the youngest of those present. They were in the stage known as 'coortin',' and ever since leaving town some half hour before they had been unobtrusively dropping in the rear of their party. They were walking along with their arms round each other's waists, and her head drooped upon his shoulder. Contrary to the rule among the Northern peasantry, who are for the most part hard-featured and uncomely, perhaps owing to the admixture of Scotch blood in their veins, the girl had the true Celtic type of beauty, straight features with black hair, and large blue eyes fringed with dark lashes, a tall figure, and a firm and well-developed bust. But the young man beside her overtopped her by a head, straight-limbed, with a broad sun-tanned face and a wide laughing mouth; the damp of the plough-land had not yet got into his bones nor the bend of the scythe into his knee-joints. They walked in silence, content to be together; your rustic has not too many words to spare to

waste any even in his courting.   But the blood
coursed none the less hotly in the veins of both.

The rich, who have more room in their houses,
and fewer constraints to trouble them, do most
of their love-making indoors.   The poor have
to do theirs in the open air, chiefly, as now, in
the long evenings coming home together from
market.   The middle classes are more restricted
by space and convention on both these sides,
which perhaps partly accounts for their higher
morality.

An Irish laborer's cottage of two rooms has
to accommodate a whole family, the younger
children often sleeping in the same bed with
their parents.   From thus herding together, and
from the necessities of country life in connection
with animals, the children are brought up in
familiarity with aspects of life which never
come under the notice of those bred in towns.
And yet the Irish women have a high reputation
for chastity; and justly, for they rarely take a
lover outside of their own class.   Within that
class they are protected by their religion; if
anything goes wrong between a man and a
maid, the priest always hears of it, and marries
them on the spot before worse can happen.

11

Generations of this restraint have bred an ingrained habit of continence among the people, so that now in the Roman Catholic districts of Northern Ireland an illegitimate child is an almost unknown disgrace.

' What did ye buy in town the day, Paddy?' asked the girl, with the intonation of a tender speech.   The limits of her vocabulary did not admit of a nearer approach to lovers' talk than the practical details of housekeeping that bore on their projected marriage.

' Them two pigs in the ass-cart, an' the Saints alone knows whether I'll be fit to kape thim through the winter.   A shillin' a day, an' not ivery day at that, isn't enough to kape a man, let alone a wife an' two suckin' pigs.   I only git two shillin' when I'm ploughin' or mowin', an' them machines is cuttin' us all out; they git all the wurruk these times.   I'm thinkin' I'll jine to larn the use av them be next year; there's no man hereabouts as knows the thrick av it, an' I've a consate that siveral av the farmers would jine an' buy a mowin' machine right out instead av hirin' them thramp wans, av they had a man as cud use it.'

' But yous is the boy as has the head,' said

the girl admiringly. ' I 'm glad I 'm to be married to yous. I 'll niver want for bit nor sup, I 'll hold ye.'

' It 's that same that 's botherin' me this minit, Norah darlin'. Whin are we to be married? It ud be ahl right wi' the house an' the wee bit farrum; but me brother Mick is that set agin you I don't know what 's kim over him. An' I 'd as lave not ang-er him. For Mick 's right fond av me the whole time, whin ahl 's said an' done.'

'Ay, troth is he; he thinks the sun rises an' sets an yer elbow whin yous is not by.'

' I 'm clane moidhered what to do. What did you buy, swateheart? '

' I 'm worse agin nor yous. I on'y got five shillin' for spriggin' an' stockins as tuk me a fair fortnight. But I scraped enough ha'pence together for a churn; an' I said as how yous wud bring it home the nixt time ye had the ass-cart in town.'

In these marriages it is the woman's part, where possible, to supply the household utensils necessary to set up house together, the man's to find the live-stock and keep a roof over their heads by his labor.

'It's comin' on saft, let's take shelther,' said Paddy presently.

'Ah, what signifies that dhrap? It'll on'y be a shower.'

'An' yous in yer new jacket an' hat wi' the red feather till it; it'll be ahl shpoilt. As it isn't goin' to last, it's ahl the more raison not to git wet to the pelt for nothin'. Let's git in behin' this ould wall for a wee taste; it's gran' shelther, an' the brackens right saft to set an.'

The girl resisted for a time, but finally, when she felt a large drop splash on her nose, her fears for her finery triumphed over her native modesty, and she let herself be persuaded against her will. Paddy calmly 'tossed' the loose stone wall, making a gap of a height sufficient to let her pass over it, and they took refuge under the ruined gable of an old church beside the road. The bracken grew thickly up to the foot of the crumbling wall; the overhanging ivy cast them into deep shadow.

'Ah, quit,' exclaimed the girl presently, in a tone half-angry, half-alarmed. 'Quit now, I'm tellin' ye. What for are ye squeezin' me so tight? For the love av Mary, Paddy darlin,' what are ye doin'? I didn't think it av ye,' and her voice died away in a murmur of passion.

When the shower was over, they rose and resumed their journey in silence, walking apart, one on the grass on either side, with the roadway between them.

When they had thus travelled a mile, the girl said timidly, —

'Pathrick.'

'Ay.'

'It's my turn to confess to Father Brady come Sunday.'

For another five minutes there was a silence, then the man said shamefacedly, —

'Norah.'

'Ay.'

'There's no call to say nothin' to the praste about yon. I'll tell him to call us for the first time in chapel on Sunday. Come an' giv us a kiss, darlin', an' make frinds agin. Troth it's all wan, whin we jine to be married so soon.'

PART II

THE BROTHERS

'THRAMP it out, Paddy, thramp it out, ye scutt ye. D'ye call that buildin' a haycock? Putt a good head ahn it. Av ye lave the hay loose yon road at the edges, the first skift av rain will get in ondher it, an' go right to the heart av it, an' ye 'll be havin' the whole clamjaffrey hatin' on us.'

'Ah! houl yer whisht, ye long-tongued divil, Mick. Give us a dacent lock at a time, an' don't go pokin' the fork in me eye. Ye nearly had me desthroyed yon time.'

'Fwhat for are ye buildin' it ahl crucked now? Ye 've guv it a tilt to the North like a thrawler in a shkite av wund or a load of turf in a shough.'

'An' why for no, ye cantankerous owl' shkibareen. I done it for purpose, the way it might lane agin the blast that comes up them hollys. Av ye put a prop or two ondher it, it 'll be as firrum as a house.'

'To blazes wi' ye, Paddy; ye 've got too many consates in yer head ahlthegither. Make the butt livil and stiddy an' the top straight an' ye can't betther it. It 's temptin' Providence ye are to send a lock of wund from behin' an' toss it on us.'

'Providence is it? Gahn! kape a civil tongue betune yer teeth. Ye have too much to say for yerself be half. Build a cock is it? Yous as can hardly tell a cock from a bull's fut. Stan' from ondher till I slither down.'

'Where 's the ropes now? I 'll hold ye that ye niver twisted them, an' divil a thrahook on the groun' to do it wid, nor so much as a sally rod to make wan.'

'Now ye 're too fast enthirely, Mick. The ropes is ondher the wee grass cock at yer fut. Go to the other side an' catch a hoult av the ind when I toss it to ye. Are ye ready? Make it tight. Ah! lift man, can't ye? Put yer shouldher into it. An' now agin for the other wan. That 's well done anyway.'

'What matther to have yon wee taste saved, when there 's half av an acre shuck out, an' a whole wan in the swathe, an' it lukin' like a shtorrum av rain ev'ry minute.'

'Now quit lamentin'. God sees ahl, an' it's time to knock aff for dinner. It must be well ahn to one o'clock, the sun's straight over the tower an' the hill. Shtrike yer graip in the groun' an' come an' down to the well.'

'It's well ye minded to bring the dinner itself. I would n't putt it past ye to forget even that. Where war ye last night? At the spriggin' camp, I'll be boun', stravaguin' about afther them girls.'

'Ay, divil a where else. But I'll be accountable to no man for me goin's.'

'There's no call to flare up now. It only shows ye've bin coortin' that Norah Sheehan agin, an' afther I've towl ye times out av' min' I won't have it. Maybe ye'll tell me where ye intind to putt her whin ye've got her.'

'You to hell with yer havin's. There's room in the house for ahl, an' I can arn bread for both av us. We're to be called in chapel come Sunday, so there.'

'Room in my house, divil a hate! An' where ud I be, I'd like to know?'

'Your house — I like that whin me father lift it betune us on his last deathbed. An' who's got a better right to live in it than me own wife an' no beholdin' to yous?'

'Ay, that 's right enough betwixt us two, but not when other folks is by. Ye 've got to prove it. I 'm yer eldher brother, an' it 's ahl mine be rights. Where 's the paper ye have to show for it? an' my wurrud 's as good as yours an' betther, so putt that in yer pipe an' smoke it.'

'You chatin' hound, you thry to best me out av me fair rights, an' I 'll be the death av ye, so I will.'

'Them 's nice wurruds to use to yer eldher brother, ye onnathural young limb. Though I would n't put it past ye to murdher me; ye 've thried it before now. D 'ye mind the day ye threw me aff of the cliff? But whether or no, divil a fut will that girl putt in my house. It 's bin a respectable house up to now; an' if ye thry to bring her to it, out ye 'll both go, you an' your trollope.'

'Say that wurrud agin, ye scutt. Say it agin, I darr you.'

'Ay, I 'll say it as aften as I like, an' I say agin now to yer face, that neither you nor yer trollope will ever set fut on flure of mine from this out.'

'Then take that, ye ignorant fule. Ye wud have it. Maybe it 'll larn ye to kape a still tongue in yer head,'·shouted Paddy. In his rage the landscape swam blood-red before his gaze, he plucked the hay-fork from the ground behind him, and plunged it into his brother's chest. The sharp steel prongs drove through bone and muscle with a grinding sound, and stood out a handsbreadth behind his back. The base stopped with a thud against the breast-bone. There was a shrill scream, the scream with which the strong man's soul rends itself apart from the body; he rocked and swayed for a moment, and fell stiffly upon his back, his arms outspread. The handle of the fork stood erect, vibrating in the dead man's chest.

The young man put out his hand to grasp it, but it started away from him with a tremor, and he leaped backward, thinking it had come to life. What was that word? Murder. It appeared to be written in letters of brass across the heavens, and all the hills around were thundering it in his ears. For a long time he stood there with his eyes fixed straight in front of him, and the perspiration pouring in streams from his body.

'He dhruv me to it,' he muttered; 'he dhruv me to it.'

It had been coming to this for a long time between the brothers, though neither of them had seen it. The nagging tongue of the elder and the uncontrolled temper of the younger made them an ill-assorted pair. Once in boyhood Paddy, in a fit of anger, had pushed his brother off a cliff into the sea, and in an agony of contrition had leapt off after him. Neither was hurt by the fall, and they swam contentedly together to land, and there fought till neither of them could stand. Since then it had gradually been getting worse. A word and a blow was a daily occurrence between them, and latterly the blow was dealt with whatever instrument came handy. It had come to be only a question of sufficient provocation and a deadly enough weapon, and that was bound to happen which had now happened. This time no remorse would avail. His brother had gone where he could not follow him.

As the young man stood there beside his dead brother, a dull strange sense of the injustice of it all began to rise and swell in his bosom. He could n't understand it. An ordinary quarrel, resulting in not quite the ordinary way, and two lives were sacrificed and

a third ruined forever.　God help poor Norah!
It was not fair.　What good did it do to any
one? and why had he and Norah been selected
for this thing to happen to?

After a long time he woke from his trance
with a start, and keeping his eyes carefully
turned from the pool of blood that was slowly
drying in front of him, he ran swiftly to the
house, as though to escape some temptation
that was behind him.　Quickly he put the
horse in the cart, and standing up in it, drove
at full speed to the town.　Down the hill of the
main street he rattled, as one of the neighbors
said, 'as if the devil was behind him,' and
pulled up with a jerk at the doctor's door.

'Docther dear, hurry for the love av God,' he
said; 'ye're wanted badly out at Michaelstown,
there's a man kilt.'

Then he walked across the road to the police
station opposite, and said to the sergeant in
charge, 'Me an' me brother was havin' wurruds
in the three-cornered field behind the house,
an' I've shtuck the graip into him.　I'm
thinkin' it's kilt him I have, an' I've come to
giv' meself up.'

ORANGE AND GREEN

THE crowd surged and muttered. It was extraordinarily still for an Irish mob. No man spoke to his neighbor, but all kept their eyes steadfastly fixed on the vanishing lines of the railway; nevertheless, through the whole mass there ran the troubled undertone, the uneasy stir of a ground-swell in the Atlantic. Every minute men came dropping in by twos and threes and took their places in the serried ranks, till the cut leading to the railway station of Lisnamore was packed from end to end with two banks of solid humanity, leaving a broad avenue down the middle. Each man, as he fell into his place, bent his eyes upon the horizon, and assumed the same attitude of tense and feverish expectation.

It was the twelfth of July, the anniversary of the Battle of the Boyne. The manufacturers of the distant town of Belrush had selected the

Northern day of rejoicing to give a holiday to
their mill-hands, and by some unlucky chance
the workmen had chosen to spend the day by
the seaside at Lisnamore.   Two train-loads of
them were coming — six hundred Catholics and
six hundred Protestants.   So the Catholics of
Lisnamore and the surrounding districts were
now assembled in their thousands to express
their disapprobation of the indecent presence
of Orangemen in their town upon that day.
Every fist held an ash-plant or a blackthorn.
stick, and every pocket was filled with jagged
pieces of limestone.

Suddenly a rumor — a whisper — flashed down
the ranks and died out like a sigh: 'The polis.'

The rhythm of disciplined feet crept upon
the ear; and the dark-green tunics and brown
rifle-barrels of the Royal Irish Constabulary
rounded the corner and came into view.   Amid
a silence of death they marched steadily up
the centre of the avenue — twenty-four stalwart
men and their officer — and behind them rode
the resident magistrate on his big roan horse.

Straight up the cut they strode, until they
reached the mouth of the station-yard, and
then came the order sharp and decisive, —

'Right wheel! — Halt! — Front turn! — 'Tention! — Ready! — Fix swords! — With buckshot — Load!'

The policemen were now between the crowd and their approaching victims. The two lines of glittering bayonets rose aloft in the sunlight; and as the snap of the rifle-breeches ceased upon the sullen air, the magistrate raised his voice and said in a dry, official tone, —

'I call upon this meeting to disperse.'

No one moved.

The magistrate then took off his hat, and, looking intently into the crown of it, proceeded to read the Riot Act, which he had printed on the lining. He gabbled through his duty with a meaninglessness born of frequent repetition.

When he had ended, the crowd laughed. But it was an ugly laugh, with the sough of a winter storm through it.

Fitzgerald, swift to recognize the temper of a mob, and loth to begin a conflict which, once started, no man might say how it would end, glanced hastily round him.

His eyes were attracted by an unexpected sight, and remained fixed. Round the corner of the road furthest from the station came a pair of horse's ears, and they were decked with orange lilies.

A big man standing opposite Fitzgerald in the crowd, the centre of a group of men in dark-blue jerseys, who looked like fishermen, followed the direction of his gaze, and exclaimed, —

'Troth, I wud n't be the man what's behin' them orange lilies for somethin'. The boys will tear him limb from limb.'

Slowly the ears lengthened into the shape of a fat cob, foreshortened by the turn, which paced sleepily along regardless of the throng; he drooped his head, overcome by the noonday heat, and shook it from time to time at the flies, with a rattle of his bit. Behind the cob came a small phaeton, and in the phaeton was sitting a young girl; she carried a knot of orange ribbons on her whip, and in her breast a cluster of the lilies.

As the girl drove deliberately forward, she flashed indignant glances from side to side. Abreast of her, along the face of the rows, there wavered a ripple, as though each man had a mind to hide himself behind his neighbor's back.

'Holy Mother! it's Miss Kitty,' ejaculated the big man.

'Miss Desmond,' said Fitzgerald, with a gasp of relief.

Kitty Desmond was the daughter of the vicar of the town, and in spite of being a Protestant, was beloved by the peasantry for miles around. Even more than by the assistance she was always the first to render them and their wives, she was endeared to the men by her beauty, her high spirits, and her winning manner. She knew every man, woman, and child by name upon the countryside, and always had a friendly word and a cheerful smile for them. She was loved by the women, but the men worshipped her. She had an absolute recklessness and abandonment of temperament which dominated them. For, except when supported by others, your peasant is prone to be cautious. She was the only soul in the town that thoroughly knew them, and the only one that dared to cross them in their blackest moods. In fact, she was at heart a coquette, with the fearlessness of a coquette. She did not disdain to practise her fascinations upon the meanest of them all. She knew

12

her power and enjoyed it, and they enjoyed
it too.

She halted her pony now opposite the police
force, and, standing up in the carriage, addressed
the mob in her cheerful, audacious tones.

'Now, then, boys, you need n't think that I
don't know what you are doing here; for I do.
And what you 've got to do is to go straight
home. So, go!'

There was an automatic movement in the
crowd, as the habit of obedience to her asserted
itself, and for a moment the meeting was on
the point of dissolving. But then the sullenness
of their temper returned upon them: the men
stood fast, shuffled their feet doggedly, and
upon their brows gathered the brooding obstinacy of the Celtic character.

Kitty watched the success of her experiment
flicker and die out. Then the blood surged
hotly over her face and neck. She was not
used to having her influence questioned, and
here where it was needed, as it had never been
needed before, it had failed. She was General
enough to recognize that her best chance lay
in a direct command. She had staked all upon
a single throw — and lost.

She knew better than anybody there, even than Fitzgerald himself, the danger of the mood that could make these men resist her, and she grew sick with apprehension. For she could see no possibility now of averting a great riot, in which probably many lives would be sacrificed. For herself, she did not stop to fear, and at least she would utilize her woman's privilege and give them a piece of her mind.

As these thoughts flashed through her brain, she stood upright, still leaning upon her whip; then she began to speak again, but this time her voice was cutting, and her face was white and scornful, —

'And you call yourselves men?' she said; 'you gather here with sticks and stones, and lie in wait for unarmed and unsuspecting holiday-makers. If they were as many as you are, you wouldn't dare to touch them. You never have the pluck to fight unless you are two to one, or get the chance of kicking a man when he is down. If you want to fight fairly, why don't you throw away those sticks and stones, and use your fists like men? But you don't want a fair fight, not you. Shall I tell you

what I think of you? I think you are mean,
cowardly savages!'

She left off, gasping, with the tears of indignation in her throat, and a hoarse threatening
murmur rose vaguely round her.

'Oh, you need n't think I am afraid of you,
you miserable idiots,' she said, with infinite
scorn. 'I only hope they 'll — they 'll knock
hell out of you,' and she stamped her foot
viciously.

'Ah, be aisy now, Miss Kitty,' implored the
big man; 'shure, the boys are only afther a bit
ov fun.'

'And is that you, Dan Murphy? You hulking
scoundrel, and you dare to look me in the face?
What business have you here, I should like to
know?'

'Troth, Miss, I 'd like nahthin' better nor to
be ahlways lookin' you in the face. For it 's
fine an' purthy,' declared the giant, skilfully
turning her flank.

Kitty's heart was softened by the blarney
of the good-natured fisherman amid the pre-
vailing rebellion of her subjects; she got out
of the phaeton, and walking up to him, laid
her hand upon his sleeve, and said, —

'Now, Dan, dear Dan, you'll get them to go away, won't you, for my sake?'

She looked up at him with a pleading gaze in the violet eyes beneath their fringe of long, dark lashes, eyes that had melted many a stouter heart than poor Dan Murphy's.

'Ah, now, Miss Kitty darlin',' he stammered, 'ye know that it's yersilf can do more wid the boys than any wan bar the praste, an' he's not here the day; foreby, he's backin' them up. Divil a hate wud they heed me. They'd as soon ate me as luke at me if I crossed them.'

'Dan, you're just a soft lump,' she spat the words at him spitefully, and returned to her seat.

Seeing that her mediation had failed, Fitzgerald now came forward and said, 'I am afraid this is no place for you, Miss Desmond, and I shall have to ask you to go home, if you don't mind.'

'But I do mind,' she replied pettishly; 'I'm going to stop here.'

'But,' said the D. I. perplexed, 'you can't. You forget what a difficult position you are putting me in. If any harm happens to you, your father will hold me responsible. And your presence here hampers me in the performance of my duty. For God's sake, be reasonable,' he concluded in despair.

'I am reasonable,' she replied in a defiant voice, 'perfectly reasonable. I don't stir a foot from here. If those brutes want to throw stones, they must stone me too. And if you want to shoot them, you must shoot me too.'

'But this is absurd,' replied the officer, angrily taking hold of her horse's head to turn it; 'I insist upon your leaving this at once.'

At his action a murmur arose from the listening crowd, and two or three voices cried menacingly, —

'Quit a hoult ov her, or we 'll make yous. Ye can just let her be.'

She was their idol, and though, like all savage worshippers, they might trample her under foot themselves in the heat of their fury, meanwhile they would let no one else touch her.

Fitzgerald turned his eyes upon them, and regarded them tranquilly; it was no part of his policy to precipitate a conflict before it was absolutely necessary. Once it began, he knew that his handful of men would be immediately swamped. Meanwhile there were

all the chances of the fickleness of an Irish
mob, and every chance counted. But, on the
other hand, it would be absolutely fatal to let
them imagine he was afraid of them. He said
to Kitty disgustedly, —

'Very well, I wash my hands of you entirely,'
and strode gloomily back to his men. Then
he drew his forces à little further off. She
would be safer by herself.

Once more every one settled down to wait.
A strained hush prevailed. The midges buzzed
round the horse's ears. No sound broke the
stillness but the rattle of a bit, the clink of
a cleaning-rod, or the grinding of a rifle-stock
in the roadway as a policeman shifted his
position, except the vague rustle that is in-
separable from the breathing of a great
multitude of men. The white limestone dust,
ground into powder beneath so many feet,
hung in a halo about their heads; throats grew
dry and parched; and close packed beneath
the sweltering heat of the sun the crowd began
to give up the strong odor of humanity. And
still the train tarried.

At last it was more than ten minutes late,
and a faint sprout of hope began to push its

head into Fitzgerald's thoughts. He had telegraphed to the excursionists at the junction that the town was up, and advised them to return home. Perhaps they had taken his advice.

Hardly was the hope born before it was destroyed. A jet of smoke spouted upon the horizon; a cry went up of 'Here she comes;' and the grip upon ash-plants and blackthorns tightened.

'Mother av Moses,' said Dan, 'but yon's a powerful long thrain. There's two injins till it, wan in the middle. Av them's ahl Orangemin we'll cop a most thremenjeous hammerin'.'

The train steamed deliberately into the station, and behind the gates of the barrier there rose the clamor of many voices, and the tread of innumerable feet. Gradually the confusion died down, words of command could be heard, and the procession could be felt arranging its order.

Outside every man held his breath. There was only one question now left to decide. Would this first train contain the Protestant or the Catholic contingent?

Every mouth was opened, and every arm

was raised — to shout if the green banner came forth, to cast if it were orange.

The gates were thrown open wide. And out of them came two banners. And one of them was green, and one was orange.

In the silence the clash of teeth could be heard, as the jaws of the crowd snapped with disappointment. But the arms still remained threateningly aloft.

Kitty drew her pony to one side, and the ranks of police parted in the midst and fell back upon either hand.

Down the centre of the avenue the bearers of the green and orange banners marched shoulder to shoulder, their eyes fixed vacantly on the horizon. Behind them came eight fife players; every alternate man had a green favor on his breast, and every alternate man an orange favor; they looked steadfastly in front of them, and strode forward with their heads on one side tootling for all they were worth. Next came two big drums; and one was decked with orange streamers, and one with green; the drummers walked side by side, and banged each more lustily than the other. Then more fifes and kettledrums, and lastly came the procession. Twelve men abreast with linked arms, green alternating with orange, with the even tramp of an army they marched resolutely forward, and looked neither to the right hand nor to the left.

The feeling of townsmanship had triumphed over religious difference; the two trains had joined; and the two processions had come forth mingled in one. To harm the Protestants now it would be necessary to attack the Catholics; and the two together made a formidable mouthful.

Still in dead silence down the centre of the avenue they went. And the mood of the crowd wavered to this side and to that. But when the banners had nearly reached the head of the cut, that sense of humor which is never far distant from an Irish mob rose to the surface, and a great wave of laughter broke and surged down the banks of men.

High above the tumult rose the roar of Dan's great bass, —

'Troth, they have the laugh ov us this time anyway. Three cheers for the Belrush boys.'

The crowd yelled, then broke and rushed in upon the procession, and smote the band upon the back until it had no breath left in it, and carried it away to have a drink. And they all trooped off to the shebeens and public-houses, orange and green together, and got royally drunk after their kind.

But now that the crisis was safely past, Kitty sat in her phaeton and wept as though her heart would break.

ANDY KERRIGAN'S HONEYMOON

'THERE's Andy Kerrigan, the crathur, in the yard,' said Anne the cook. 'He lukes just starved wid the could, an' it an Aist wind that ud cut ye in two, an' him just afther buryin' his wife the day.'

'Well, take him into the kitchen and give him some dinner,' said I, seeing what was expected of me.

'Did ye ever hear him tell how he come to jine an' marry her?' she asked, lingering at the door.

'No.'

'Thin ax him to tell yous. It's worth hearin'. For he's a cure all out, so he is,' and she departed.

Andy Kerrigan was a half-witted creature, a kind of handy man about town. He hung about the steps of the hotel, and did odd jobs, cleaned cars, and drove them occasionally when he got any one to trust him with a horse. Before her death his wife had taken in washing, and they rubbed along together in a hand-to-mouth style, which is not uncommon in Ireland, by the help of a little charity and an occasional relapse upon the 'Poor-house' when times were hard.

When I entered the kitchen a quarter of an hour later, I found Andy just finishing his dinner. He had a large bag of Indian meal beside him, and was sitting on a three-legged stool inside the wide open chimney-place in front of the turf fire upon the hearth; the hard black turves standing perpendicularly in serried rows sent forth a grateful heat.

'A power ov thanks to ye, sirr,' he said, 'for as good a male as iver I ate, an' may ye niver come to want yersilf. Your wans was always kind to the poor: many 's the dinner I 've had in this same kitchen, an' many 's the day's whitewashin' I done till it,' he added, looking significantly at the smoke-blackened walls. For your Irish peasant never misses the opportunity of a stroke of business.

'Here 's some tobacco for you,' I said hastily, to turn the subject, handing him a plug of Irish twist.

'Thank ye kindly,' said Andy, and at once bit a corner of it off and shoved it in his cheek.

'Don't you smoke?' I inquired.

'I do, I smokes an' I chaws. But chawin's best. It's both smoke an' mate; a taste o' tabacca stays the stummick more nor anythin' else ye cud mintion. Many's the long day's wurrk I done on a plug o' that same twist.'

'And where did you get the bag of meal, Andy?'

'Ah, that, is it? Troth the Crowner gave it to me. Ye see it was this road. Me an' Mary Anne, that's my wife, was a wee bit happy-like 't is a fortnight come Sathurday, an' we come to wurrds, an' I just putt her out av the dure an' left her there, an' it sames she caught a could an' niver rightly got the betther ov it. For she died o' Monday. An' the Crowner's jury they sat on her, an' tould me I was a crool husband; but I niver mint no harrum, it was just a bit ov fun. But the Crowner he sint me the bag o' male afther the funeral the day. They do be sayin' that in his house the gray mare's the betther harse, but I know nahthin' about that. On'y he sent me the bag o' male, so he did.'

'Yes, I heard you had lost your wife. That's sad news. You'll miss her greatly, I'm afraid,' I said, seeing that my scruples were wasted, and I need n't trouble to avoid the subject. The poor like to dilate upon their woes.

'Troth will I,' replied Andy with a heavy sigh, 'I don't know what I'll do widout her. She cud boil spuds wid any wumman I iver seen, cud she. An' there's more nor me that will miss her, now I'm tellin' ye; the town will be hard put to it for their washin', I'm thinkin'. Oh deary me, I'll niver git anuther wumman to come up to her, I'll niver git another Mary Anne.'

'I'm afraid not,' I assented, looking at the bent and wizened figure of the old man; then I continued, 'But I hear there's a story about your marriage. What is it?'

'Ah, there's none ava,' he protested, evidently pleased; 'it's nahthin' whatever, but I'll tell it ye. It was in the days when I was young an' soople. Ah, the days whin we was young, the days whin we was young, there's nahthin' to aqual thim. I'd just got me discharge from the militia at Lifford, an' I came prancin' into town fit for anythin' from murther to chuck-farthin'; there was nahthin' I cud n't do.   I had a whole pun note in me fist, an' a consate of mesilf that I wud n't ha called the Quane me ant.

'Well, I come clattherin' down the Back Street goin' to buy the town wid me pun note, whin who did I see but Mary Anne Murphy drivin' the cows out ov Mrs. Flanigan's byre.   She had no shawl to her head, an' her feet was as bare as the day she was born, an' I won't be sayin',' he added, with a reminiscent twinkle in his eye, 'that she was overly an' above clane.   But the red hair of her — Ah, man, it blazed like the whins on all the hills on Bonfire Night!

'An' the notion just tuk me, an' I says to her, says I, "Good morra to ye, Mary Anne Murphy, will ye marry me?"

'"Do ye mane it?" she said.

'"To be sure I do," says I.   "Why for no?"

'"Sartin sure I will," she says, says she.

'So she sput in her han' an' hel' it out to me, an' aff we wint togither to find the praste, an' left the cows to stravague aff to the field their own swate way.

'Father O'Flatherty he was havin' his

breakfast whin we come in, an' I says to him, "Good-morra to you, Father, we 're come to be marrit."

'"Marrit," he says; he was takin' a drink ov tay at the time, an' he splutthers it ahl over the flure. "Git out wid yer practical jokin' makin' me choke over me tay. Git out ov my house before I take me horsewhip to ye both."

'"Ah be aisy now, Father," says I, "it 's not jokin' we are. We 're in sober arnest."

'"Is it argy wid me, yer own parish praste, ye wud, ye onnathral varmint. I tell ye, I 'll not marry ye, an' that 's flat."

'"Thin be the powers," says I, "marrit or not marrit, I 'll live wid Mary Anne, an' she 'll live wid me, an' you 'll be the cause of immorality an' scandal in the parish. Ye wull, won't you, Mary Anne?" says I.

'"I wull," says she, grinnin' ahl roun' her head.

'"Ye two divils," says the praste girnin' at us, "for that 's just what ye are. Ye 'll be sorry for this day, I promise you. I 'll marry you, an' I cud n't wish worse to neither of you, for I don't know which is the warst. Ye 're both as mad as leppin' sterks, but it 's betther

13

maybe to mix the blood nor spoil two dacint stocks. The Lord sind ye won't have no childher," says he, the ould haythin, an' we niver did to this day.

'So thin he calls the sexton, an' the foor of us proceeds to the chapel roun' the corner, an' us two was marrit.

'"Thank ye kindly, your Riverence," says I, "an' what may I be owin' ye for the job?"

'"Twenty-five shillin'," says he.

'"An' how many shillin' is there in a pun?"

'"Twenty," says he.

'"Mother av Moses," says I, "but mathrimony 's the egsthravagint business all out. Here 's me pun note, it 's ahl I have in the wurrld, an' I 'm thinkin' I 'll have to be owin' ye the other five shillin'!"

'"Ah, I 'll forgive it ye this time," says he. "But don't come here axin' to be marrit no more. I 've had enough of ye."

'"Ahl right, yer Riverence," says I, an' out me an' Mary Anne goes.

'"An' what will we do now?" says she.

'"I niver thought o' that," says I, "but I s'pose we 'd betther go on home to me mother, and see what she 'll say to us."

'"D'ye think she 'll take us in?"'

'"Well, I know she 'd be right glad to see me home from the sojerin': she 's powerful fond av me, she thinks the sun rises an' sets on me elbow, but I 'm not so sartain about yous. But we can only thry; she can't kill us anyway."

'"Where is it?"'

'"Five mile out along the mountain road."

'"Luck's till us," says she, an' off we starts. But the further we wint, the more onaisy in me mind I became, till whin we came into the lane that led to the house, I says to Mary Anne —

'"Mary Anne, darlin'," I says, "I think it ull be betther for you to wait outside av the dure, while I break the news gintly. Av me mother 's by her lone, it ull be ahl right; but av me sisther 's there, too, it 's the divil ahl out."

'As luck wud have it, the first sight I claps eyes on whin I come in at the dure is me sisther, Casey, sittin' in the chimney corner, the oul' catamaran, an' I knew there 'd be wigs an' the green before ahl was done.

'"Arrah, Andy, me jewel, an' is it yersilf?" says me mother runnin' an throwin' her arms round me neck; "but it 's a brave lad ye 've grown, an' it 's right welcome ye are home from the sojerin'. Troth it's a sight for sore eyes just to see ye."

'"Yis," says I, "I'm home, an' I'm not alone. I'm marrit. Come in out of that an' show yersilf, Mary Anne."

'Mary Anne came in, an' me mother an' me sisther just lets wan shriek, an' I shouts, —

'"Run, Mary Anne, run for yer life."

'They turned and grabbed the two three-legged stools they was settin' on, an' me an' Mary Anne cleared the flure wid wan lep, an' was out an' away down the back lane as hard as we cud tear, an' them two weemin gallopin' afther us an' screaming like hell's delight. But me an' Mary Anne was young an' soople, an' we ran like hares till we came to the edge of the bog. And thin I says, —

'"Houl' an," I says, "let me go first," an' I tuk the path across the bog that lay betwixt two big bog-holes.

'Well, me sisther, bein' the younger, comes first to the edge of the bog, an' she was that blind wid fury she cudn't see where she was goin', an' whin she come to the first bog-hole souse she goes intil the middle of it neck over crop, an' I caught a sight of her legs goin' up

in the air wid the tail ov me eye, an' down I
sits, an' thought I 'd ha shplit.

'Well, whin we was sore wid laffin, we wint
on back to the town, an' the last we saw of the
pair of thim Casey was lyin' wid her arms on
the bank of the bog-hole an' me mother haulin'
at her ahl she was fit to dhrag her out.

'But whin we came to the town it was
dhrawin' near han' night, an' there was the
greatest goin's on iver ye seen. We was met
at the head of the town by a crowd of the boys
that was out lukin' for us; for the praste had
tould on us, and they 'd been sarchin' ivery-
where for the bride an' bridegroom, they said.

'So they took an' cheered us, an' carried us
roun' the town. An' they had the town band
behind us, wid wan big dhrum an' six little
wans, an' fourteen flutes, an' they banged and
tootled till they cud n't bang nor tootle no more, .
an' the street boys yelled, and the dogs yelped,
an' there was a noise thro' the town ye cud n't
hear yersilf spake for the best part of an hour.
Glory be! it was a weddin' fit for a king,' and
the old man spat reflectively into the fire, as he
looked back upon that crowning moment of
his life.

'An' whin it was ahl over, "Mary Anne, honey," says I, "I'm hung-ry; I have n't had nahthin' to eat the day since me brackfast, an' that graspin' oul' praste has copped ahl me money, have ye iver a pinny?"

'"Divil a thraneen," says she, "but just wan ha'penny."

'"A power o' use that is to stay two hung-ry stummicks upon," says I, "but I tell ye what. We'll do things in style the night if we niver did before nor since. We'll have an illumination to light the way to our bridal couch."

'So we bought two farthin' candles, and wint to slape in the hay in Mrs. Flanigan's byre.'

'On the principle,' said I, 'of *qui dort, dine*.'

But that remark was lost upon Andy.

A PAUPER'S BURIAL

'OUL' Shan the Pote,' as the townsfolk called him, was a descendant in the direct male line of Shan O'Neill, the great rebel of Queen Elizabeth's day. He had a fine pedigree, but little else; for of all the possessions of his forefathers, all that remained to him was an old battered, silver punch-ladle and a silver-mounted dirk with a cairngorm in the hilt of it, which the envious-minded amongst his neighbors declared to be a bit of yellow glass. At such insinuations Shan used to wax mightily indignant, showing that he still retained his pride of birth; but on ordinary occasions that feeling was entirely subordinate in him to two others — his belief in his own genius as a poet, and his overflowing love for 'me daughter Kathleen, what 's in Australey, the crathur.'

His actual position in the social scale did not quite coincide with his high ancestry and

literary pretensions.   He was a stone-cutter by
trade, and had been for some years at one time
in his life in my grandfather's service as odd
man.   With the partisanship of the Irish
peasant, he thought that the latter circumstance
made the family in general, and me in particular,
his peculiar property, and used to treat us
accordingly.   When he was a young man, and
the sap was still effervescent in him, he had
been in the habit of going an occasional 'tear;'
and once my grandmother, seeing the recumbent
form of a man very drunk sleeping peacefully
in the middle of the road in front of the house,
and having a vision of carts jolting over him,
called in the police to remove him to the lock-
up.   In the morning it turned out, much to her
dismay, that the man she had thus given into
custody was Shan, whom she was called upon to
go and bail out again.   That was the standing
joke of his life.   Whenever he saw her in his
latter days he used to say, ' Ah, now, misthress
dear, don't be ang-ery an' go an' give poor oul'
Shan up to the polis, bad scran to thim,' and
then he cackled vehemently at his own wit.   ,
    The last time I saw him was when I was a
schoolboy of fifteen home for the holidays.

He was then a little thin old man with deep
wrinkles in his face, and long wispy gray hair
that used to blow round his face in a dishevelled
halo. I can see him now ambling along the
street of the little town with his eyes fixed
straight in front of him, with the inward gaze of
the poet and the dreamer; 'moonin' down the
road like a jackass wid a carrot in front of his
nose,' his persecutors, the street boys, used to
call it.

When he was more than usually elated by
the recent appearance of some piece of doggerel
of his in the poet's corner of the local rag, he
would be heard crooning over to himself with
a curious kind of sing-song lilt the words of his
great poem, that had made his local reputation,—

> 'Oh, the banks an' braes o' wild Kilcross,
>   Where the blue-bells blow
> An' the heath an' fern an' soft green moss
>   In the springtime grow,
> Where the lads an' lasses take their play
>   Of a Sunday morn,
> An' the blackbirds sing the livelong day
>   In the rustlin' corn.'

When I used to point out to him that 'the
rustlin' corn' was a pure myth of his imagination,
as the cliffs of 'wild Kilcross' were as bleak a

place as you would find in 'a month of Sundays,'
and that not a blade grew anywhere within a
mile of them, he used to reply, 'Ah! whisht
now, can't ye? If them wans haven't got the
sinse to plant a lock ov oats, is it me as ye'd
blame for it? Ahl that the likes av thim has a
mind for is shpuds.'

But his favorite haunt where I could always
find him at need was in the churchyard under
the shadow of the square, ugly tower of the
barn-like church, amongst 'the beautiful uncut
hair of graves.' At that time he did very little
work, and used to spend the greater part of his
day there stringing rhymes together, while he
renewed the inscriptions upon the old weather-
beaten stones, and made them once more
legible; for the lapse of time and lichen-growth
make those memorials of us in stone hardly
more enduring than human life itself.   There I
used to seek him out with offerings of snuff, to
get him to tell me those stories of the ancient
grandeur of his race which I loved to hear; for
youth has always a tinge of snobbishness, which
is at the root of that hero-worship common to
all children.

But Shan's mind was fixed on other things.

He would parry my inquiries by bringing out a roll of old newspaper cuttings, which he always carried about with him, and use me as an audience for the lack of a better, spreading the precious morsels out on the flat tombstone on which we were sitting, and holding the fluttering paper down with a thumb on each corner as he read them aloud, although he knew every word by heart. Or he would say, as he chipped away at his labor of love with deft strokes of the hammer on the head of his chisel, —

'Tell ye how I knew that oul' ladle really belonged to the great Shan O'Neill, is it? Well, this is the way ov it, d'ye see? Min' the shparks, sonny, or they 'll be flyin' in yer eye. While I 'm thinkin' ov it, did I iver tell ye the shtory of the road Kathleen an' yours kim to be thegither. It was whin yous was a wee fellah, a weeshan roun' roll of fat in yer perambulator, an' ye kim down to the big meady wan day whin they was puttin' in a shtack of hay; I mind it was the year afore I got the toss off of the cart of hay, an' tuk harrum in me innards, an' I was niver the same man afther; an' ahl the quality from the big house was there havin'

a picnic, an' Kathleen she was a bit slip ov a
gurl ov thirteen at the time, an' she kim to help
carry the tay. Well, yous an' she made great
frien's, an' ye rouled in the hay an' covered
aich other up till many's the time ye were
shtuck be the forkers ahl but. An' whin
they tuk yous home in the evenin', Kathleen
she started to roar an' to cry afther yous, an'
there was no houlin' her; we thried ahl we
knew to quiet her, but deil a hate wud she quit,
an' her mother was fair moidhered wid her, an'
at last she ups an' takes her in unner her shawl,
an' walks her ivery fut ov the road up to the
big house, an' lan's her in there at ten o'clock
ov night, an' she ups an' says, says she, to the
misthress, as bowl' as ye plaze, "Mam," says
she, "ye've made Kathleen here that conthrairy,
yous an' that babby ov yours, that there's no
houlin' her. I'm fair broke wid her, so I am.
So I've brought her up till ye, an' ye must just
kape her, for I can do nothin' wid her." An'
the misthress she laughs an' says, says she,
"Well, if I must, Biddy, I shuppose I must.
Must is a harrud worrud," says she; an' so
Kathleen she shtops from that day out in the
house an' luks afther yous. I min' well she

used to wheel ye in the perambulator, an'
many's the time she shpilt ye in the shtreet,
but devil a hate did yous care, ye just rouled in
the gutter, an' laughed till she picked yous up
agin.   An' she shtayed as long as yous was
there, — she was terrible fond ov yous; it bet
ahl iver I see.   But when yous was eight year
oul', an' she was goin' on near han' twinty, an' a
fine han'some soople lass she was too, glory be!
They tuk an' sint yous away to school in
England, an' she was that lonesome afther
yous she was neither to houl' nor to bind, an'
she just tuk a notion, an' she ups an' she emi-
grates to Australey.   An' she was there in service
for foor year, an' she wint wid wan and wid another, an' no wunner, for she was the purtiest
gurl in the foor baronies, an' at last she marries
a squatter-fellah out there, an' now I hear tell
she has a grand carriage an' servants galore to
her back.   But she does n't forgit her oul' daddy,
she's not the wan to go for to do that; but she
sinds me enough ivery month to kape me at
me aise like a lord wid lashins ov tobaccy, an'
shnuff, an' tay, an' shugar.   But ahl the time she
thinks a power ov yous till this minit, more be
a dale, I'm thinkin', than ov her oul' man him-

self, as she calls him.   Many 's the time she 's
axed me to go out till her, but I would n't lave
the oul' place even for her; I 'll lay me bones,
plaze God, where I spint me youth.   May the
saints purtect her, and may her children stan'
by her as she has stud be her oul' father an'
mother.'

At this point in the story the old man always
found it necessary to see in which direction the
clouds were blowing, and I took diligently to
making out the rest of the inscription upon
which he was at work.   He told his story all
in a breath, and always in the same words, as
a parrot might, from long habitude.   It was
the old story of Irish emigration.   Sons and
daughters, not content with a fare of potatoes
and tea and a futureless outlook at home, drift
off one by one as they grow up to different
parts of America and Australia; there they
form new ties, and forget the old folks at home
and all they owe them.   In this case one of
the daughters did not forget her debt; and, as
rarely happens in this world, it was the most
prosperous and best beloved of all who was
thus mindful of her old parents and supported
them in their age.

It was seven years before I revisited the sleepy little town, and I had heard nothing of old Shan for a long time. The day after my arrival I went for a drive on a hired car; the Jarvey was the same old character that I remembered from my youth up, but I had outgrown his failing memory; the mare was the same old screw, only a little grayer and scraggier than of old. She was painfully climbing the steep hill just outside the town, when she suddenly stopped in the middle and turned round her head to look at us.

'Ah, luk at that now. She says she's tired, the crathur, an' wud like a rist,' cried her compassionate driver with the familiarity of a privileged class. 'Shure yous is in no hurry. What 'ud ail ye?' and he got down and put a stone behind the wheel to keep the car in position, while we surveyed the view.

Opposite and behind us another hill rose steeply, even more precipitous than the one we were on, which had proved too much for the mare — a green knoll crowned with the gray old church, its summit fenced with the back wall of the churchyard. Along the strip of level ground on the dividing line, from which the twin hills sprang, wound a gray ribbon of dusty road; and as we watched, a singular procession crawled slowly along its length below us.   Four old men in the light blue workhouse uniform painfully bore a long oblong black box upon their shoulders; behind them followed two old women, also in light blue.   It was a pauper funeral.

' Luk at yon now.   Troth, there 's a sight ye wud n't see the like ov anywhere outside of the foor baronies, an' mebbe ye might niver see agin,' said the driver, with a complacency in this unique local spectacle evidently bred by the remarks of previous strangers.

As he spoke the procession halted at a stile, from which a footpath sprang straight up the hill to an opening in the shoulder of the churchyard wall: it led to the portion of ground outside ' God's Acre ' allotted to those outcasts, who, by venturing to die within the walls of the ' Poorhouse,' forfeited that last right of miserable humanity, a resting-place in consecrated ground.

The old men rested their burden on the stile and grouped themselves round it.

' ' What are they doing now ? ' I asked.

And the driver replied, ' They 're fittin' the rope till it. Them oul' flitters is n't fit to carry a heavy corp, lit alone the coffin, up yon brae, the crathurs, so they tie a rope till it and dhrag it up.'

The group opened out and resolved itself into its parts as it slowly climbed the hill. First came two old men bent double, each straining at a loop of rope passed over one shoulder and across their chests; behind them jolted the coffin, to which they were harnessed, over the uneven ground; next came the other two men as a relay, ready to relieve their comrades when tired; and behind them the mourners, the two old women.

I now noticed that the path was composed of three parallel lines upon the green sward. On each side was a footway, worn smooth and bare by the feet of the men and the following mourners. In the middle was vaguely outlined a strip less distinct where the grass was beaten down like a pock-marked field of oats after a rainstorm, and was thinned and straggling like the hair upon a head beginning to grow bald. That was the mark where the coffin was dragged.

14

'Whose funeral is it?' I asked, with a pity-
ing sigh at this outrage upon the dead.

'Oul' Shan O'Neill's,' came the startling
answer; 'he was a stone-cutter, and a gran'
han' at the pothery; he cud write a pome as
fast as another man cud mow a fiel' ov hay.
Troth cud he!'

'But I thought his daughter kept him.'

'Holy Post-Office, how did ye come to know
that?' exclaimed the driver, in surprise at the
unexpected extent of my information; 'that was
Kathleen, the wan dacint wan ov the whole
bilin'.   She kep' him till a year ago.   But thin
she lost ahl her money in wan ov thim banks
in Australey, and the other childher' wud n't
give no help, and so the oul' man come on the
parish, an' he niver hel' up his head from that
day out, and now they 're buryin' of him.'

And so the descendant of all the O'Neills
was haled at the end of a rope to a pauper's
grave.

THE GAUGER'S LEP

THERE was agitation in Kilcross. For years
the fishing industry of the place had been
deteriorating. Steam-trawlers owned by English and Scotch firms in Liverpool and Glasgow
had gradually come to infest the bay, and
tugs came twice a week to relieve them of
their takings. The primitive appliances and
means of transport of the native fishermen had
left them unable to cope with this competition;
so that it was with difficulty they could get
their fish sold, and often it was left to rot on
their hands. Further than that, the huge beams
of these new-fangled engines disturbed the
bottom of the bay, raked up the spawning
beds, and interfered with the habits of generations, so that no man knew where to look
next for the fish.

But all that was going to be altered now;
the press had taken the matter up and interested

itself on behalf of this distressed class; busy-bodies who saw an opportunity of gaining a cheap notoriety for themselves wrote to the papers and caused questions to be asked in Parliament.   The result was that relief works had been undertaken in the shape of a boat-slip, with a jetty to protect it from the weather, and to form a harbor for incoming boats.   Up to this time the open beach had been their only landing-place, and dragging the heavy boats over the rough shingle every time they were launched or taken out of the water had not tended to increase their lasting qualities; while often, when it was at all rough, it was impossible to land at all, and a sandy cove further round the coast had to be sought out.   So now, with a placid gratitude to Providence, all Kilcross was sitting on the shore watching the first stone being laid.

For weeks afterwards the new works afforded great employment for eye and tongue to the inhabitants of the little village.   In the reunions on the beach or round the fires at night in the cottages, there was no other subject of conver-sation but ' the gran' new kay; ' and when there was nothing else to do, the large square stones lying about came in handy to sit upon and smoke a pipe while watching the masons at work. Some of the men even went the length of earning an occasional day's wages by helping to transport the stones to their resting-places; but the general opinion was that, when everything was being done for them, it was unnecessary to jog the elbow of Providence, and that such sustained energy as regular work entailed could not be expected of a people used to the precarious calling of the sea.

Presently the works were finished, and the idlers' occupation was gone. The particular busybody who took the credit to himself for all that had been done, broke a bottle of champagne over the new pier and made a speech. The fishermen quite believed him when he told them that they were very fine fellows; but with the narrow shrewdness of their class, thought that he was rather a fool to take so much trouble over other people's affairs that did not concern him, for they did not know how it served his interest to do so.

On the following Sunday morning, a lovely day in the late Donegal summer, when the women and the younger men were preparing to set out for chapel, the word went round that ' the fish is in the bay,' and in a moment all thought of devotions was abandoned. First there was seen a dark-blue ripple on the surface of the water, coming rapidly nearer, and shot with flashes of silver in the sunlight; this was caused by the ' sprit ' or small herring-fry leaping out of the water to escape their natural enemies. Above them hovered screaming flocks of gulls; every now and then one of these would mount to a height, and sheathing its wings, would drop with a splash like a stone into the water, emerging with a small fish in its beak. Hard upon the track of the ' sprit ' followed shoals of shehans, glascon, whiting, mackerel, herring, and pollack; after them came porpoises, dolphins, and seals; conger-eels twined themselves among the wrack along the rocks lying in wait for the fry; and even a whale was seen spouting in the offing. The larger fish devoured the smaller, only to be themselves devoured in turn by others.

In a moment the nets were got out and the boats launched. The women and boys remaining on shore armed themselves with baskets and seine-nets. With these they rushed into the

water up to the waist and lifted out baskets
full of the fry and even of the mackerel, which
sometimes ran themselves up dry upon the
beach in their eagerness after their prey.   A
shoal of mackerel entered the mouth of the
little harbor, and a seine-net being quickly
stretched across the entrance, not one escaped.

That evening there were rejoicings in the
little village.   Enough fish had been caught
in that one day to salt down and last them
through the winter, leaving a handsome sur-
plus to hawk through the inland towns and
villages.   The whiting had been caught in such.
numbers that no one had any use for them, and
they were left to rot in heaps upon the shore,
until the country people came with carts and
drew them for manure.   But the old men shook
their heads, and said it was a bad sign for the
weather; they had never known so plentiful a
take, and the fish must be flying before some
prodigious storm.

Upon this occasion the croakers proved right
for once.   For when the people awoke two
days later, they found that the first of the
equinoctial gales was upon them before its
usual time.   The clouds were scurrying in

huge banks across the sky, and the sea, turned leaden-gray, was running violently shorewards, beaten flat by the furious force of the wind, and breaking upon the beach with a low moaning sound. As the day progressed the wind abated slightly and allowed the waves to rise, and they roused themselves in their might and beat upon the devoted pier. For a time their efforts were unavailing, for the back that it presented to them was encased in concrete and proof against assault; but at last a huge roller launched itself over the top of the pier and fell upon the stone-work in its centre; the mortar, impregnated with the salt air and the spray, had never had a chance to dry and get properly hard; the force of the water, gripping the edges of one of the huge stones in the centre, whisked it from its feeble hold and carried it hurtling into the sea beyond. The waves laughed, exulting in their success, and hurled mass after mass into the breach thus begun, churning stones and mortar up in a circular whirlpool, until by evening there was a huge round hole in the new pier reaching to the bed-rock beneath.

Meanwhile the sights and sounds of wrecks

at sea were beginning to be apparent. Minute-guns were heard in the offing, the reports almost drowned in the rush of the storm; a three-masted vessel went ashore on the opposite side of the bay under the lighthouse upon St. John's Point, and could be seen rapidly breaking up. Masts of vessels, beams, and pieces of wreckage began to come ashore, brought by the set of the currents and the force of the wind. All the fishermen were gathered upon the beach apathetically watching the destruction of the quay, from which they had hoped so much, and on the look-out for prizes.

'What's yon?' presently said Big Dan Murphy, the leader of the group, pointing to a dark object tossing among the surf. They formed a line joining hands, and he dashed in and pulled it ashore. It proved to be a cask of rum.

'Lend a hand, boys,' he said, 'to take it up to me shanty, an' we'll have a sup the night whin ahls over.'

Nothing further came ashore, and the night saw a dozen men gathered in Murphy's hut. The village stood a little back from the beach in a dip of the land that sheltered it from the boisterous fury of the Atlantic gales; but Murphy's hut stood alone on higher ground and nearer the sea, the sentinel and outpost of the rest.

The men sat round the open turf fire upon the hearth, each with a tin porringer in his hand, and the cask in their midst.

'It's well that the ould gauger's gone,' said one with gloomy satisfaction, 'or he'd be pokin' his ugly nose into this. He always kim down on the night ov a storrum to say what had kim ashore.'

'They say,' replied another, 'that this man is worse agin. New twigs swape clane an' he's for iver drivin' aroun' the counthry wid his trap an' his little wee black pony.'

As he spoke there was a knock at the door, and the gauger stood in their midst.

'How's this, boys?' he said. 'What have you got here? Your name's Dan Murphy, isn't it?'

'Ay, till the bone breaks,' returned Dan briefly.

'Don't you know that this doesn't belong to you? Flotsam and jetsam belongs to the Crown and the owner of the land upon which it is washed ashore.'

The other men looked anxious, Dan dogged.

'Findin's is kapin's,' he said; 'I niver hear tell that the open baich belonged to no man. I pulled yon barrel out ov the say at the risk av me own life, an' I've as much right to kape it as any man else, an' what's more, I mane to kape it.'

'I've heard of you, Dan Murphy,' replied the gauger sternly, 'and you'd better not give any trouble. I'm not the kind of man to stand any nonsense. I seize this rum in the Queen's name.'

In an instant he was on his back on the floor with two men on top of him; but the red-bearded gauger was a strong man and a bold, and struggling fiercely, he gave vent to a shrill whistle. The door burst open, and in rushed six policemen, whom he had brought, expecting resistance. The biggest of them made at Big Dan, but found more than his match; the giant stepped lightly aside, and catching his assailant as he passed by the scruff of the neck and the waistband, he swung him round with the impetus of his own rush, and hurled him back through the door the way he came.

Then seizing an axe that stood in the corner,

he shouted above the uproar, ' If us is to git no good ov it, no man else will neither,' and he brought down the axe on the head of the cask, smashing it in and overturning it.

The rum gurgled placidly out of the hole, and ran in little streams about the floor, forming a pool round the gauger where he lay on his back, and soaking into his clothes; above him the fight raged fiercely, the men whirled close-locked in the narrow space of the hut. Presently a rivulet of rum meandered gently into the fire upon the hearth, and immediately the floor of the hut was intersected by rivers of blue flame. The rest of the combatants rushed stamping and swearing out of the hut. The gauger still lying on his back could not see what had occurred; and thinking that the others were escaping, he grappled his two assailants more fiercely to him, so that they could not rise. In a moment he was an island in a lake of fire, the flames lapping his sides, fastening upon his clothes, and licking his beard. With a yell of surprise and pain he released his opponents, who fled shouting from the hut. He rose and rushed after them. But the flames had caught, and were fanned to fury by the gale.   He threw himself down and rolled upon the ground in agony, but they had got firm hold of his rum-soaked clothes, and relit in one place as fast as they were extinguished in another. At last he could bear the torture no longer, and uttering shriek on shriek, he rushed headlong down the slope a pillar of towering flame, and threw himself over the cliff into the sea a hundred feet below.

When he was pulled out a few minutes later he was a mere mass of charred cinder, hardly bearing any resemblance to humanity, and with only a few sparks of life left in his body.   Before he could be carried to the nearest hut he was dead.

For their share in his death Dan Murphy and the other two men received long terms of penal servitude, and the scandal consequent upon the incident cast a blight over the little place.   No further relief works were undertaken.   The jetty is now in ruins, but a hundred yards off along the cliffs there is a spot still pointed out as ' the gauger's lep. '

THE GILLIE

THE snow had been lying for several days, when I woke one morning and found my windows covered with the delicate tracery of hoar-frost. 'What a day for snipe-shooting!' I said, and jumping out of bed, sent a message to Hughie M'Nulty to come up at once, that I wanted him for a day's sport.

Hughie was a professional angler, who gained a good living during the summer months by acting as guide and assistant to rich English salmon-fishers, and hibernated for the rest of the year by the help of any odd jobs he could pick up. He was my constant companion on my vagrant shooting excursions, and a livelier, more talkative, or more interesting companion could not be wished for. He arrived, buttoning up his coat, before I had finished my breakfast; and after he had cut some sandwiches and filled my flask with whisky, we set out together.

' Now, Hughie,' said I, before getting clear of the town, for I knew of old his little weakness for cheating the revenue, ' have you got a game license yet this year? '

' Troth, Misther Harry, ain't I own keeper to Misther Donovan ov the Castle, an' d 'ye think the likes ov him wud begrudge me a dhirty license? '

' I doubt you 're too emphatic, Hughie, to be quite truthful. If you like to confess while there 's time, I 'll get you one. But, remember, if you get caught by the gauger without one, I 'll not be responsible, and you 'll have to clear yourself as best you may without my assistance.'

' God sees that, if it 's not the truth that I 'm tellin',' said Hughie, and we turned off the road into the fields.

Presently my companion remembered he owed something to his dignity, and began : ' I tell ye, surr, ye were lucky to git me the mornin' at ahl, at ahl; ivery wan was fur havin' me ahl to wanst. There was Misther Donovan sint down for me, jist afther I got yer message, wantin' me to go and shoot cock with him on the island in the lough; and there

was Misther Fitzgerald, an' Dennison, an'
Kilpathrick, an' Dawson, an' Gorman — they
was ahl jist ravenin' for me; but I wud n't
disappint yer ahner for one av thim, an' I jist
ups an' towld thim so.'

'You 've made a bad shot this time, Hughie;
you should name some one that I don't know.
I was playing cards last night with all those
gentlemen, and I know that not one of them
can go out shooting to-day.   Mr. Donovan has
gone up to Dublin this morning; Mr. Dennison
is going to the fair at Enniskillen; Mr. Fitzgerald is on duty; Mr. Kilpatrick has a case
coming on at the Court-house; and the other
two can't leave the Bank on a market day.
You should really be a little more careful of
your ground, Hughie.'

'Ah, kape wide, can't ye, an' houl' yer whist.
Ye 'll be havin' the burds as wild as hawks, an'
we won't git inside of an ass's roar ov thim the
day.   Ye might as well have brought thim
dogs ye wanted, scuttherin' through the snow,
if this is the road yer goin' to kape jabberin'.
There, what did I tell ye?   Auch!   Begob, I
thought he was clane away,' and Hughie ran
forward to pick up our first snipe.

' Now, I'll take ye to a place that's jist
swarmin' wi' them this weather. D'ye know
the ould bog of Tubbernavaicha — the well in
the bog, that manes — foreninst the face of the
hill beyant? No? — well, that's the place
ye'll fin' them.'

When we came to the old bog we recognized
the fact by finding the surface sinking beneath
our feet, and the icy water oozing into our
boots; otherwise, there was nothing to mark
it from the surrounding country beneath its
winding sheet of snow. As we got further and
further out the ground became more and more
tremulous, and we sank to our knees at every
step, but luckily for our comfort the frozen
mud and snow had caked into a hard mass a
foot below the surface; the whole bog shivered
and sank at each fresh step as we crashed
through the thin upper crust of ice, but we did
not go through the solid mass below, and it
rose buoyantly again beneath us like a life-
buoy in the sea. But still we did not come
across any birds.

' This bates ahl, this bates ahl,' Hughie kept
muttering to himself. ' Not a burrd in the
whole bog; but there's just the wan wee spring

in the middle that we're comin' to.   Luk out,
surr.   Ah, well shot!   Ye'll soon larn to shute
av ye kape on.   The way he wint straight
away behin' us I didn't think ye cud turn to
git a shot at ahl, an' yous shtuck up to yer
knees in the dirt.   But we're in luck the whole
time not to be in deeper; for I've seen the
time I've thramped this bog an' it's cum up to
me arrum-pits in every part ov it, an' I've had
to sweem the pools with me gun over me head.
Troth, we'd be friz enthirely av we had to do
the likes ov yon the day.'

 'Well, Hughie, I don't think much of your
hot corner.   Can't you do better than this?'

 'Well, ye see, it's this way, yer ahner, in the
harrd weather the burrds takes to the springs
av runnin' wather.   I thought the bog wud be
saft enough for thim still, but I was mistook.
But we've got thim now, anyways; for I was
on the jayological survey what cum down here
from Dublin 't is three year cum Michaelmas:
I helped to hould the tapes, an' av I didn't larn
nothin' else, I larnt the springs to fin' the
snipeses through ahl the counthry.roun'.'

 As he spoke a snipe got up in front of him,
and flew slowly and hungrily away along the

surface of the snow. Hughie blazed both barrels at it with no effect. ' Ah, I knocked a hatful of feathers out av that boy, anyway,' said he, looking after it indignantly; and as it was just topping the wall of the next field, I brought it down with a fluky cross-shot. He walked forward and picked it up in disgusted silence, and did n't speak another word for a good half hour.

At the end of that time we walked into a wisp of eight, out of which we got a brace each, and Hughie's good humor was restored. ' Did ye see the way them two of mine wus shot?' he said; 'the wan that wint towerin' straight up in circles, an' thin shut his wings an' fell with a whop that wud have shuck the breath out av his body av he 'd had any lef', was shot through the heart; the other wan flew a wee bit wid his head thrown over his back an' his wings fluttherin'. I knew he wud n't go far; he just soothered down slantways wid his wings straight out — he was shot in the head. Ah! is n't it just like thim, the divils, to rise like that ahl av a plump; why cud n't they cum wan be wan, singly an' giv' a dacent man a chanst at them? Mother av Moses! but I laughed, yer ahner, when ye wiped me eye a while back foreninst the stone wall.'

The laughter had not been perceptible, but this was making the *amende honorable*, and to show there was no ill feeling I handed him the flask to take a drink. 'An' what about lunch, surr?' he said, as he handed it back.

'We'll go up to the top of that hill and have lunch now.'

'What for wud we climb the brae? There's nothin' up there batin' a rabbud mebbe.'

'I want to see the view.'

'Auch, the view,' said Hughie, in high disdain; he did not see why any one should go out of his way to climb a hill when he could stop comfortably at the bottom.

Arrived at the top, the wide prospect below us repaid me at least for the journey. The country spread white and glittering before us until it met the gray line of the sea upon the horizon, the faint undulations of the stone walls looking like infants' graves, and the few hedges and trees on the bare landscape draped with waterfalls of snow.

Hughie, on more practical thoughts intent, searched out a well of spring-water and un-

packed the sandwiches out of the game-bag.
Just as we began to eat, a bird flashed round
the corner of the wall and flew straight away
from us down the hill. 'Shute, man, shute,'
cried Hughie, dancing with excitement; I
crammed my sandwich into my mouth, and
seizing my gun with one hand, let it off vaguely
from the hip.

'What's the good in telling me to shoot and
scare the bird when it was out of range already,
you idiot?' I said.

'Oh, niver min' the range. What's a pen-
north ov powdher? Ye shud ahlways shute
at a wudcock if it's in the same parish wid ye.
Ye'll niver git another chanst,' and he pointed
to where the bird was winging its way with the
steady flight of an owl across the open to the
opposite hill.

'Tell me, Hughie,' said I, when we had settled
down to our lunch again, 'why don't you learn
a trade to work at in the winter, and then all
you earn in the summer would be clear profit?
You must earn a good deal then if you only had
constant employment to keep you going the
rest of the year.'

'Ay, I do that. I arn me guinea a day an'

live on the fat ov the lan', but the best ov the
saison is on'y for two months, an' the rest is
slack.   Whin I wus a bhoy me father sint me
to Ameriky to larn a thrade, an' he giv me the
time ov day in me pockit; but I kim back agin
widout it, an' niver a tatter but the clothes I
stud up in, an' thim in rags, an' since thin I
niver thried to larn a thrade agin.   Ye see, it 's
this way, surr, some rivers is early, an' some is
late, an' what wid wan an' another there 's
fishin' for them as likes it from the beginnin'
ov March to well-nigh the ind of October, an'
that on'y laves foor months ov the year empty,
tho' I 'm not arnin' reglar ahl the time.   Sometimes I 've gone over to Glasgy an' Liverpool
in the winter an' dhrew me thirty shillin' a week
workin' on them stamers; but as soon as the
time cum roun' I started to hanker afther the
oul' life; there 's no life like it.   I 'd give
the swatest song that iver wumman sung for
the song ov the tight line to the music ov the
reel, so back I kim.   I kin fish an' I kin shute,
an' what more do I want?'

   ' That last is a matter of opinion,' I said, ' but
the sarcasm was too English, and passed harm-
lessly over his head.

'Why don't you marry and settle down?' I continued, 'and you'd soon get regular work.'

'Marry, is it? Me? I'd luke a nice gomeral, wouldn't I, wid a parcel ov childher trailin' at me tail. Me, I've got as much call wid a wife as a pig wid a side-pocket. The whisky's done, an' none to be had nearer nor Biddy M'Intyre's shebeen, two mile away, an' it on'y putcheen; but putcheen's none so bad whin there's nothin' else handy, an' the hollys roun' her house is just crawlin' wi' snipeses.' And Hughie turned the flask upside down regretfully

I took the hint, and said, 'Very well, then, we'll make for Biddy's. But how is it that there's a shebeen left in this part of the country? I thought that the priests had stamped out the illicit liquor trade hereabouts.'

'Ay, so they have. But, ye see, Biddy's a Protestant, an' can snap her fingers at them.'

'Then there's some advantage in being a Protestant, after all.'

'Ah, what's a sup of putcheen to a quiet min', av yer a Protestant ye have to bear the load av yer own sins instid av the prastes bearin' it for you, an' givin' ye a wee bit penance ivery now an' thin. Av I was yous I could n't lay quiet in me bed for thinkin' ov me sins.

'Talkin' ov Ameriky,' continued Hughie, for once started talking he never stopped, 'there's Annie M'Gay kim back from it Friday's a week that fine that ye wud n't know her. I wus seein' her yistherday, and axed her if her tay wus to her taste, an' she ups an' says, says she, "The shuperfluity ov the shugar has spoilt the flavoracity ov the tay." Boys, but she's the gurl wot can use the gran' long wurruds,' and Hughie rolled the syllables over again lovingly in his mouth.

'That minds me,' he continued, 'ov a day we had yestherday's a month. It was a fine day, the Duke of Donegal was havin' a shutin' party, an' me an' twinty others was the baters. A broilin' day it was, an' we got a drouth on us ye cud cut wid a knife. The Duke he's a fine hospitable man, an' he giv us a barrel of porther for lunch, an' as much as we cud ate wi' lashin's an' lavin's to spare. An' we finished the porther betwixt us, an' was fair sighin' for more. Whin we kim to Farmer Gavigan's, an' he axed us in an' giv us whisky all roun', beautiful whisky it was, it wint down that soft, like mother's milk.

But the head-keeper he hears of it, an' he comes up rampin' an' ravin', an' he says, says he, —

' "Farmer Gavigan," he says, "I 'm surprised at yous, givin' these men whisky on the top ov porther, an' thim just foamin' for a fight."

' "An' why wud n't they fight?" says Farmer Gavigan; "ducks will go barefut."

' "Troth, they 'll khill other."

' "Ah, lit them khill away," says he; he 's a fine raisonable man is Farmer Gavigan.' And Hughie licked his lips at the luscious recollection.

' D' ye min' the day,' he went on, ' that ye caught the salmon on Lough Legaltian?'

'No, and you need n't start any of your lies about it, for I never caught a salmon in my life.'

' Ah, thin it was yer brither; it 's all wan. Boys, ye shud ha' bin' wid us the day him an' me caught the big throut. There was a big sthorrum on the lough that day, an' we wus blown clane aff ov the wather, an' dhruv five mile down the lough to the far end ov it. About half-way down yer brother he shtuck in the throut while throllin' the flies afther the boat, an' if it had n't bin for him we 'd ha' bin ahl drownded for shure. The waves wus

that big, an' kep follerin' that fast, that
they 'd hav overtuk us an' swep clane over
the boat, for we did n't know how to row fast
encugh, but that throut started on ahead, an'
sind I may die if it 's not truth I 'm tellin',
but he towed us afther him as if he 'd bin a
whale.'

'It must have been a good strong trout line
that you had that day!'

'Ay, the best; ov our own sellin'. It was
that light an' thin ye cud see through it ahl
but, but ye cud houl a man up be it. Well,
when we got into the shelther of the bay at
the far ind I started to gaff that throut, but
he wus so big I cud n't lift him into the boat.
Yer brother had to git a catch ov him be the
gills an' be the tail an' help me to take him
in. An' whin we came to weigh him he was
a hundred an' ten pound, every ounce of it,
an' he wus foul-hooked be the tail.'

'Why not make it the even hundredweight
at once?'

'Now ye think it 's jokin' I am, but I 'm not,
an' I can prove it to yous, that same. For
I had the head stuffed, an' it 's in me chimbly at·
home this minute.'

' All right, I 'll come in and see it to-night on our way home. I should like to see that head.'

' Ah, now ye spake ov it, I mind me I sint it on'y yistherday's a week to the Fisheries Exhibition in Lunnon.'

' I thought so. It 's a wonder I never heard of that trout from my brother.'

'Ah, him is it? He 's got as much mouth on him as a cod.'

' Damn,' said I, 'there 's the third snipe I 've missed since lunch, and I did n't miss one at all before that. My eyes are all watering.'

'I 'll tell ye what it is, Misther Harry; it 's them specs ye hav on. They catch the glare ov the snow. When yer eyes was fresh ye saw everythin' distinct agin the snow; but now they 're tired ye 'll see nothin'. So ye may jist giv up.'

' I suppose that 's it. I know that last night I did a thing I never heard of being done before. I shot a snipe by moonlight.'

' Now ye 're sayin'.'

'It 's a fact, you unbelieving Jew; you 're so accustomed to hear lies roll out of your own mouth that you don't know the truth when you hear it. I was coming back in the evening about eight o'clock, and there was bright moon-light; as I was passing through that rushy bit at the head of the town a snipe got up in front of me; I got it clear against a snow bank, and bowled it over as clean as if it had been day-light.'

'It's as well we're at Biddy's now; I'd as lave hav a dhrink afther that. Bring out the putcheen, Biddy.'

The old woman brought out a large earthen-ware jar from underneath her bed, and taking down a couple of delf mugs off the dresser, handed them to us.

'Will you have a half-un or a whole-un?' I asked.

'A whole-un, to be shure, an' another on the top of that. Here's luck, more power to yer elbow. There's no call to be puttin' wather in it; it shpoils the flavor an' lits out the hate.'

The flavor was a strong taste of turf smoke, and the spirit was so fiery that it nearly rasped the skin off my mouth and throat on its way down.

'An' whin yous hav done that, I'll larn ye a wrinkle. Just put a glass of the crathur in aich ov yer boots, an' ye won't know yersilf; it 'll kape yer feet that warrum an' yer boots that aisy. It 's ivery bit as good as dhrinkin' it an' betther, an' it 'll save yer inside in the mornin'.'

I did so to try the experiment.

At that moment the old woman caught sight of an approaching car, and exclaimed, 'Auch, wirra' it 's ruined I am, I 'm desthroyed enthirely. Here 's the gauger comin' up to the dure wid a polisman beside him, an' me niver to notice him attendin' on yous jintlemen,' and she made a grab at the jar to hide it.

'Never mind that; it 's too late now,' I said, 'and I 'll see you through. Come in, Gillespie, and have a drink with me.'

'I don't mind if I do for once,' replied the gauger; 'a man wants something inside him sitting on a car in a day like this. It is the coldest day I ever was out in. But you must have that stuff outside the house the next time I come this way, Mrs. M'Intyre.'

Meanwhile the policeman and Hughie had foregathered in a corner, and were having a drink together; but the effect of the whisky made itself rapidly apparent, coming upon the change from the biting air outside to the stuffy atmosphere of the hut.   Presently their voices became raised, and we heard the policeman saying, —

'Stan' up agin' me, is it? ye little ginger-bread whipper-snapper ye.   I'll tell ye what I'll do; I'll put down me five pound agin' yours, an' I'll box you for twenty rounds, an' sweem yous a mile, an' run ye five, the best man to lift the hard stuff.'

'Box? is it yous?' said Hughie scornfully. 'D' ye see that little roun' button on the top ov yer saucepan?   I'll putt ye on that an' twirl ye roun' for half an hour, see that now,' and he put his leg behind the crook of the other's knee, and giving him a push on the chest, sent him toppling his full length on the floor.

Hughie looked rather frightened at the success of his wrestling trick, as the policeman rose quivering with passion; but remembering he was in the presence of his superior, the latter touched his cap and contented himself with remarking, 'Wait till the next time I catch ye, me bould buck, dhrunk in the streets, or by your lone in the counthry, an' I'll giv ye a bastin' ye won't forgit, I promise ye.'

I thought by this time it was time to go, and saying good-day, went out. As I went out I heard the policeman say to Hughie, 'By the way, me boys, suppose ye let us see your license now.'

'License is it?' said Hughie; 'what wud I want wid a license? I have n't fired a shot the day. Shure, this is the masther's second gun I 'm carryin',' and he came scuttling after me.

'Oh, but them polis is botheration,' he said, when he reached me; 'there 's too many ov them in the counthry be half; ye cud feed the pigs aff ov them ahl winter an' not fin' the differ.'

From that point home was a straight walk in along a hard level road, and we swung briskly along in the frosty air.

'Not bad walking,' said I, as we entered the outskirts of the town, 'four miles in three-quarters of an hour.'

'Walkin', says you,' replied Hughie, with impartial justice, 'it 's not us at ahl as did it; it 's the putcheen. It 's a powerful strong walker is putcheen. Thank ye kindly, Masther Harry,' and Hughie touched his cap, put his hand in his pocket, and walked away.

'THE FINAL FLICKER'

CHARLIE VAUGHAN sat playing chess with his sister, as they had played it every night these thirty years. They belonged to the yeomanry class, a class that is mostly English or Scotch by extraction, and has few Irish characteristics. In the narrow circle of their lives on the lonely farm there was not much room for variety; they did the same things at the same hour of the day from one year's end to another.

As bedtime drew near they began to quarrel. She said that he had taken his finger off a piece before altering his mind, and moving it back; he denied it, and they quarrelled. The same quarrel had occurred every night in all those years. They loved each other dearly, but the game would n't have been a game without its quarrel. She swept the pieces off the board in a passion, and he wandered gently off into the night to see that all the gates about the farm were locked and the house securely barred.

To-night he was not quite in his usual mood. Perhaps the quarrel had been a little more real than usual, and had jarred upon his nerves. The subtle seduction of the moonlight moved him. He felt a void in his life, a vague craving for sympathy, for something which he had never known. After a time he identified the feeling as one which had occurred periodically to him before. It was a yearning for one sip of the wine of life before it was too late, a sense of weariness, of discouragement at the thought that he had never known that joy which is every man's birthright once in his lifetime, the joy of knowing the full meaning of a woman's love.

Now he remembered the incident that had started the train of thought. He had been making a move, and his eyes fell upon his hand, and he had recognized with a strange outwardness for the first time that it was the hand of an old man, the fingers bent and gnarled, the nails dull, the muscles corrugated, and the veins dried up and withered. If he was ever to know more about women than he knew now, it behoved him to act quickly ere his manhood had quite died within him.

Once or twice before he had awakened to the

same fact, but never with such urgency as now. Even still he was the wreck of a fine man, and there had been a time when he might easily have found favor with women, but he had let his chances slip.   A bookworm and a dreamer, he had let his youth slide by before he knew that it was gone.   His manhood he had spent beneath the rule of his elder brother.   Once he had asserted his right to an individual soul, and fallen in love with a woman, and she was ready to reciprocate his love.   But when he went and told his brother, the elder replied: ' You can marry if you like, but as sure as you do, out you go out of my house.   There 's not enough on the farm to keep more than the three of us. I've never married, and I don't see why you should. '

For the moment his manhood rose in arms, and he determined to go out into the world and make a place for himself; but he put it off and put it off, and his brother was twenty years older than himself, and it seemed a pity to lose his chance of the farm, so the time never came, and he grew old waiting for his brother's death, and the woman that he loved grew old too.

At last his brother died, and he went to her

and asked her to marry him, but she said: ' I
loved you well once, and would have stood by
your side if you had had the heart to make a
fight for me. I 've waited for you all these
years, but now it 's too late. I 'm too old to
change,' and she died also, and they were never
married.

After her death he was numbed for a time,
for he had so little· that the loss of even the
placid affection of their later years made a great
gap in his life. Then the farm began to go
wrong; he had not the practical head to manage
it as his brother had managed it; and though he
worked as hard as ever, what had formerly
sufficed to keep the three in comfort could now
barely support the remaining two. In truth,
weakness of character had been his bane all his
life, and would be to the end. He had not the
strength to carry any purpose to its appointed
goal. He was strong neither for good nor for
evil. He was cursed with the curse of Reuben,
' Unstable as water, thou shalt not excel.' But
he knew that he was weak, and it was very
pitiful.

To-night, after shutting up the house, he went
to his bed; and as he lay awake there through

the watches of the night, his desolation came home to him and ate into his heart, and he pitied himself exceedingly.

About three o'clock, the darkest part of the night, he rose and wandered restlessly out into the garden, and sat alone there with the 'night of the large few stars, the mad naked summer night,' till its fascination entered into his marrow and stirred his placid soul with a strange disturbance.

As he sat there in the darkness, suddenly there was a movement in the hedgerows and all the trees around him, and a twittering burst forth on every side; it was the birds rousing themselves from their night's slumber. For five minutes the matin song lasted, and then as suddenly ceased, and a great stillness reigned over the world, waiting for the birth of another day. Five minutes later the first ray of dawn tinged the eastern horizon, and the birds burst into song a second time to hail the new-born day.

Often before he had noticed that sudden outburst and sudden hush before the dawn, and vaguely wondered what it meant. But the sound of cocks crowing and the wakened life of a farmyard came to his ears, and reminded him of the thread of his daily duties that had to be taken up.

When he entered the house one of the maids was already down, and was cleaning the kitchen window, kneeling upon the table, with her back to him. He went up to her, and to attract her attention laid his hand upon her ankle. He felt a sudden tremor run through her, and at the contact a flood of fire pulsed through his own veins, for the glamour of the night was still over all his senses.

She turned and looked at him with a wanton twinkle in her eye; they were bold, black eyes in a gypsy face, and he wondered he had never noticed before how pretty she was. Something in her gaze struck him. He looked at her shiftily. He wanted to take her in his arms, to ask her to kiss him, and he opened his mouth to do so; but, after all those years, the hinges of his tongue worked creakingly, the thought of taking decided action of any kind out of his ordinary groove daunted him, from long disuse his executive faculties were no longer under the control of his will, and the words that issued from his mouth were quite different from what he had intended, they were dictated by habit; he jerked out with parched lips, —

' Where 's the key of the byre, Cassy?'

' Troth, sir, you have it hangin' on yer little fing-er,' she replied, with a glance that showed understanding and a spice of contempt for his weakness of purpose.

' Oh, ay, so it is,' he answered, and turning, shuffled hastily out in confusion.

But he couldn't settle down to his work, and soon gave it up, and started for a walk in the cool morning air, hoping thus to allay the fever of his blood. All the way he was arguing with himself, despising himself for the failure of his overtures, and yet frightened at the idea of their succeeding. He tried to persuade himself that it was respect for his sister that had withheld him, but even he could not sink to such self-deception as that.

It was haytime, most of the mowing was already over, and nothing further could be done with the grass until the sun and wind had had time to dry the dew of the night. Few people, therefore, were yet stirring, no smoke rose out of the cottage chimneys, not a sound was to be heard but the croak of the corn-crake running before him in the meadow, the juicy swish of a distant scythe through the wet grass, or the strident sound of the whet-stone upon the blade. Crossing a field, he met the daughter of one of his tenants carrying two pails of foaming milk — a pretty, fair girl with a sun-tanned face. She was not the least like the other, but again the same mad longing came over him, checked by the same infirmity. He wanted to ask her to put down her pails and to give him a kiss, but, unready as ever, all he could force his lips to stammer out was, —

' Good-morning, Mary.'

' Good-morning, surr,' she answered, with a courtesy, and passed on to tell her mother that ' big Misther Vaughan' knew her Christian name — a depth of interest of which she had never suspected him before.

For some days afterwards every time he met Cassy about the house she looked at him, and every time she looked at him he made up his mind to kiss her the next. At last he met her on the stairs early one morning, and did kiss her. She made a slight scuffle, and, more from his nervousness than her resistance, the kiss only fell on the tip of her ear, and she scuttled downstairs laughing. But neverthe-less he felt uplifted in his own esteem all that day; he actually had achieved the task he had set himself.

The next day Cassy was missing, and never returned. For a time there were some queer rumors about her, which at last were con-firmed by the birth of her child. And soon afterwards, to his great dismay, he was served with an order for maintenance as the father.

Of course he went to law about it; but, as he afterwards told himself bitterly, he was fool enough to admit that he had kissed her once, and in the light of that admission the jury found against him with £100 damages.

Not long afterwards Cassy was married, and it began to be whispered about that her hus-band was the real father of the child, and the pair had taken advantage of Vaughan's sim-plicity to saddle him with the responsibility.

Mingled with their disapprobation before there had been a certain respect in people's attitude to him; they were surprised, and said, 'They did n't think Charlie Vaughan had it in him.' But now all this was changed to amusement and contempt.

But that did not affect ' old Vaughan,' as he now began to be called. He was too much taken up with his own disillusionment to mind other people's conduct. From Cassy's manner he had thought that he had at last attained the wish of his life, but he now recognized the meaning of her regard for what it really was, the mere ephemeral desire of a pregnant woman ; and he had let her see through his weakness, and himself suggested to her the means of his own undoing.

His old sense of weariness and discouragement returned upon him and settled down over his life. He saw that with the ridicule in which he was held what had now become his consuming desire, the only means of renewing his self-respect, had become utterly hopeless. His thirst for the wine of life had come to him too late to be ever quenched. He lost heart. The sap went out of him. The neighbors noticed that he failed visibly, and grew rapidly gray. Within the year he was dead, and no woman had ever loved him.

A DIVIDED FAITH

MAGGIE PATERSON stood on the edge of the frozen surface of Lough Legaltian and looked about her with a dreary sense of loneliness. Round her were several groups of chattering girls; they glanced at her furtively from time to time, and she felt that they were talking of her; she wished to speak to them, but the reputation of her father's sternness, the life apart that she had led, and the barriers of custom, which are so strong in country life, stood between them. Some of them she knew by name, nearly all by sight; but though they were of her own age and station, she had never played with them; she had never gone to school like other children; she had always lived at home with her silent, gloomy father, who thought of nothing but his religion.

Now, as she stood there, a spectator of the life in which she should have shared, and the

joyous shouts of her compeers rang in her ears,
blended with the metallic whir of the skates
upon the ice, a bitter feeling of rebellion welled
slowly up in her young heart. All the joys of
childhood and of youth, which she had never
known, all the repressed instincts of her vigorous young life, called aloud in her for outlet,
and a slowly gathering wave of restlessness, of
resentment against all the forms of her narrowed
life, swept over her.

Her eyes, bent inward upon herself, no longer
saw anything of what was happening around
her. A young man, clashing his skates together, came up and sat down near her to put
them on; he was one of many now hurrying
from their work in the winter twilight, to make
use of a spell of frost which comes but seldom
in the moist climate of Donegal. He looked
at her hesitatingly, got up, and sat down again
nervously; but she noted nothing. She saw a
vision of herself learning to know the inward
meaning of life; she felt a craving for some
being outside herself to whom she might be
necessary, for whom she might experience
some feeling other than the merely dutiful
affection which she bore to her father as a

matter of habit.   And with that vision before her fixed gaze, she moved out slowly over the lake.

When she came to herself she found herself standing in the middle of the ice, while a figure on skates was hovering distractedly about her. She looked at him, and as soon as he caught her eye, he dashed boldly up and said, —

' Good-evening, Miss; can I help you on with your skates ? '

She remembered him now; she had seen his face on the rare occasions when she passed through her father's shop; he was the manager of the drapery department.   His name was Johnny Daly.

' I can't skate,' she said pathetically, feeling that this was the last drop in her cup of bitterness.

' I can teach you, if you like,' he replied diffidently.

' Father does n't like me to be out alone.   I ought n't to be here now.   He would be right mad if he knew it,' she answered, with an exaggerated gratitude that she had at last found some one who appeared to take an interest in her.

' Perhaps you would like me to see you home then?'

'Thanks, I should like it very much later on. But I am not going home just yet. Now I am here, I intend to enjoy myself.'

The defiance of her tone was so very much out of proportion to the mild manner in which she was taking her enjoyment, that the young man felt inclined to laugh. To cover his embarrassment, and at the same time to display his skill, he began gravely to execute figures round her. Unaccustomed to outdoor exercises, the girl looked with wide eyes of admiration at his process of 'showing off.' But by this time they had worked out into the centre of the lough, where the spring which fed it bubbled up in a clear open space. In doing a backward roll he approached dangerously near the edge; she opened her mouth to cry out; at that moment his skate caught in a roughness of the ice; he fell backwards with a crash, and broke through the thin ice into the black water beyond.

Maggie screamed for help, and dark figures came flitting along the ice towards her. But they were a long way off, and she saw she must depend upon herself if the young man's life was to be saved. He came up and clutched at the edge of the ice, which broke off in his fingers,. and he disappeared again; it was evident that he could not swim.

Rapidly the girl unwound her long knitted scarf from about her neck, knotted her purse in the end of it, and flung it to him as he rose the second time.

He seized it eagerly, and gasping from the chill of his sudden immersion, said, —

' Shure you 're an angel, Miss Maggie; hold on a bit, don't pull till I tell you.'

Then he gradually broke his way through the thin ice till he came to a thickness sufficient to bear his weight.

' Now pull,' he said, and when the rescuers arrived on the spot they found their work already done, and Daly trying to persuade his master's daughter that she ought n't to shake hands with him while he was so wet.

Before the others arrived within earshot, she said to him with a motherly air, ' Now run away home and get your wet things changed, or you 'll catch cold. To-morrow is Sunday, and I 'll see you at church.'

At the church porch the next morning, at twelve o'clock, Maggie found the usual assemblage of young men sitting upon tombstones and lounging against the headstones of graves, as they watched the congregation enter. This particular morning they were massed together like a herd of bullocks eying a strange dog, and all gazed steadfastly at Johnny Daly, who was sitting on a large tombstone by himself swinging his legs disconsolately. Behind them the bare barnlike church was squatly silhouetted against the sky. When he saw her his face brightened, and he came up to her with an air of relief.

'Good-morning,' she said; 'are you coming into church with me?'

'If I may,' he replied, looking at her curiously.

'Of course,' she said promptly, and they passed into church and entered a pew together.

All through the service she noticed that he watched her closely, and copied her every movement. The rest of the congregation stared at the pew in a manner that made her feel very uncomfortable, and seemed greatly in excess of the occasion.

As they were going out together, she said to
him, —

' How is it I 've never seen you in church
before? '

' Don't you know I 'm a Roman? ' he replied
wonderingly.

Then the demeanor of her neighbors was
made plain to her, and she blushed to think of
what she had done.

' No, I didn't know; why didn't you tell me? '
she stammered. ' Why did you come in if you
did n't like it? '

' But I did like it,' he replied in a vibrant
voice. ' I 'd do more than that to sit along of
you. Didn't you save my life last night? '

Maggie blushed and kept silence, but a gentle
glow of satisfaction thrilled through her.

Presently they came to the cross roads, one arm
of which led homeward, the other to the shore.

' I 'm going this way,' she said, motioning
towards the beach.

' May I come too? '

' Of course you may,' she laughed, with a
coquettish glance at him from under her long
eyelashes; ' do you think I 'd have mentioned
it, if I had n't meant you to come?

'Does father know you're a Roman?' she inquired suddenly, after a pause.

'Of course.'

'Then how is it he keeps you in the shop? I thought he was so bitter against your folks.'

'So he is; but there's no one else in the town as can hold a candle to me at the feel of the stuff. And old Paterson — I mean, Mr. Paterson, Miss — does n't mix up his business with his religion, or he would n't be the smartest trader in the town, as he is now.'

Every Sunday after that they went to church together, and for their half-hour's stroll afterwards. She looked forward to the meeting as the one bright spot in her dull existence. Her starved heart was ripe for love; and soon her whole life became centred round the glow in this one young man's eyes. Her father knew nothing of what was happening. He attended the Wesleyan Chapel, where the service was half an hour longer, and always found his daughter at home when he arrived.

Old Paterson was a queer character in his way. His hard-featured face showed the Scotch blood that is so prevalent among the middle classes in the North of Ireland. His was a nature that had been warped by adversity. Somewhat late in life he married a wife whom he tenderly loved. After one short year of wedded happiness, she died in giving birth to Maggie. Up to the date of that crowning sorrow of his life, Paterson had been an ordinary church-goer, somewhat Low Church like the rest of his class. But from that moment onward his religion flowed in an ever bitterer and narrower stream. The emotional side of his nature, thwarted in one direction, expended itself fiercely in another. He became noted in the parish for his intolerance and rabid sectarianism. In him all the forces of Orangism, its opposition in race, class, and religion to the surrounding Papists, reached their fullest development.

Gradually his bigotry became too intense for the orthodox Church to hold him. He got himself elected a churchwarden for the mere purpose of thwarting the vicar at every turn. At last, when the harassed clergyman was nearly persecuted to death, that lack of humor which was an inherent element of Paterson's severely practical mind, delivered him from his enemy. Paterson's eye fell upon the church notice-board, and perceived that it was held in an Oxford frame, which was in the form of a cross. This was rank Popery, and not to be borne in a Protestant establishment. In all haste he summoned a vestry meeting, and proposed that the Oxford frame should have its ends sawn off and all resemblance to the accursed symbol removed. The vestry-meeting, composed chiefly of his friends, and Scotch like himself, gravely carried his proposal into effect. But the ridicule of the town descended upon the idea, and the mutilated notice-board remained for a testimony against him.

Paterson shook the dust of an ungrateful sect from off his feet, and joined the Wesleyans; he built them a tin church, and raised them into prominence. His position of patron gratified his lust for power, and for ten years now he had set the tone to the narrowest clique of the community.

All this time, however, he kept his business apart from his religion, and prospered greatly. His shop was the one place where he made no difference between a Catholic and a Protestant. But all his energies flowed in these two main streams — his business life and his religious life

— and left no particle of the rich emotion, which was their source, for the unfortunate daughter, who was growing up with a heart starved by the lack of nourishment.

Lisnamore is a hotbed of gossip — that vice of small towns and small minds — and soon everybody in the place was discussing Maggie's affair with Johnny Daly. Old Paterson himself alone remained in ignorance of it; he inspired too healthy a respect in the breasts of his neighbors for any one to approach him on the subject.

The priest, Father O'Flaherty, was one of the first to hear of the grievous lapse of Johnny Daly into church-going, and immediately seized an opportunity of speaking to that unruly member of his flock.

' You 're quite a stranger, Johnny,' he began, the first time he met him in the street; ' how is it I have n't seen yous at midday mass these last three or four Sundays? '

' I go to church,' said Johnny shortly.

' An' what call have yous to go to church, when you shud be at chapel like your forebears before you, John Daly? ' inquired the priest sternly.

But Daly was at that restive stage of a young man's passion, which takes no account of authority, human or divine. He glowered at the priest darkly, and replied, —

' That 's my business; an' I 'll do as I like. Just you show me the man as 'll cross me.'

Father O'Flaherty, alarmed at such unaccustomed violence, saw that this was a case for diplomacy, that the bonds could not be strained too tightly for fear that they might burst, and replied soothingly, —

' Oh, ay, to be sure, I mind now, they did be tellin' me there was a girl in the case. An' young blood must have its road. But don't be doin' anything foolish, Johnny, my son. I 'll be expectin' yous at chapel wan of these days.'

The priest hurried off, glad to be well rid of his ticklish mission. And where he had failed, no one else felt inclined to interfere. The months rolled on, and Johnny Daly's weekly appearance in church became too much a part of the established order of things to any longer attract notice. Scandal appeared likely to die a natural death of sheer inanition, when suddenly a breath coming, no one knew whence, fanned it into more than its original brightness, as the embers of a dying fire often spring into a fresh glow from some unknown cause.

A council of matrons was held, and it was decided that when Maggie's good name came to be 'spoke about,' it was time her father, 'poor innocent,' was told.

This delicate duty was finally undertaken by Mrs. M'Connell, a butcher's wife, and the 'mother of eleven,' one of those women who delight in arranging other people's affairs, and do it by discussing those affairs with everybody that they can get to listen. But even she stood rather in awe of old Paterson.

The next evening at teatime she attired herself in her Sunday finery, and walked across the road and knocked at Paterson's door. Maggie was not in the room when she arrived, and Mrs. M'Connell opened fire at once before her courage had time to evaporate.

'I 've come to spake to yous about yer dahter, poor innocent lamb, an' I ought to know, as is the mother of eleven, an' has brought up an' married foor dahters already, an' thim not so much as sayin' "Thank ye" wanst they are safely settled, an' me afther toilin' an' moilin' an' wearin' me fingers to the bone for their sakes. Ah, it 's an ongrateful wurrld, Misther Paterson, an ongrateful wurrld, that 's just what it is.'

Paterson perceived beneath this flood of words that there was some unpleasant news about his daughter; and with the instinct of a highly secretive nature, he set his face as a mask and stood upon his guard.

' But maybe ye 've heerd tell of what they 're sayin' about Maggie?' pursued the matron, as he made no reply.

' Maybe,' he answered vaguely. It was not his cue to give unnecessary information or encouragement.

' They do be sayin' that she 's enthirely too thick with that young Daly.'

' Ay, do they?'

' He goes to church wid her every Sunday these six months, an' him a Roman. I wonder the praste does n't hinder him. Did ye know that?'

' Ye 've told it me now.'

' An' I did hear they 've been walkin' about the lanes together in the dusk, so we thought it was time some wan tould ye the road that things was goin'!'

'That 'ud be no harm, if they was goin' to be married,' said Paterson suddenly, prompted by an utterly unexpected instinct — an instinct of protection on behalf of his daughter and of antagonism against the vulgar gossip of the town.

'Ay,' ejaculated the visitor, entirely dumfounded at this unexpected attitude in a man of his proverbial intolerance.

'I 'm thinking,' continued the old man reflectively, 'that I 'm getting past my work over and above a bit, and Daly's a likely young chap to take into partnership.'

'But he 's a Roman.'

'A Roman may make a good business man and a good husband.'

'Ay, sure enough,' gasped the lady, too astounded to say all she thought.

'And now, Mrs. M'Connell, is there anything else you have to say?'

'No.'

'It 's a pity, then, that you took the trouble to dress yourself up to come over here and try to make trouble between a father and his daughter. If I might make bold to give you a bit of advice, it would be to mind your own business more. If you looked after other folks' affairs less and your own better, your husband might n't be owin' me that twenty-five pound this minute.'

At this personal turn in the conversation Mrs. M'Connell hastily left.

But though the enemy was thus put to flight in confusion, she left no less consternation behind her. Now that his visitor was gone, the old man was quite at a loss to explain to himself the impulse which had led him to make a suggestion at which yesterday he would have held up his hands in horror. It had sprung suddenly full-armed from nowhere. Even now the idea did not possess that impossibility for him that he expected. He examined it — Daly was one of the inferior race, a Celt, a peasant by blood, and a Roman Catholic by religion, but now all those things were as nothing in his eyes. He could only remember him as the faithful servant and as the possible lover of his daughter.

That last was the idea that swallowed up all others. He thought of his own religious strictness, and it had suddenly retired very far away. The thought of his wife, and through her of her daughter, was nearer him to-night than it had been any time these twenty years.

What was it that had roused these old memories, this sudden tenderness? He asked himself this question, and found the solution in the mysterious manner of his visitor; he had not permitted her to say all that she had come prepared to say. What was this evil that threatened him?

In the ordinary course of affairs the old man would have spoken to his daughter at once; but this uneasiness determined him to see for himself, first of all, how matters lay.

That night was Saturday, and he avoided Maggie all the evening. In the morning he followed her when she went to church, and found himself, for the first time for many years, sitting behind the pew where the two lovers were sitting together, where he and his wife had once sat in the days that now came back so freshly to his memory.

Maggie's profile, with the sun shining on it, was the very image of his wife; and his heart grew yet softer as he noticed the confident droop of her little head towards her lover. Nor did the devotion with which Daly watched her every motion escape him. He stole softly from the church, feeling as though he had suddenly grown very old, and that he had lost something out of his life which he had never troubled to make his own, but which he had nevertheless expected to be always there when he stretched out his hand to gather it. Now that the first place in his daughter's affections was lost to him forever, he suddenly discovered its value. But he was a strictly just man, and recognized that he was himself entirely to blame for the loss that he had sustained.

He felt very tired, and sat idly in his chair, his hands resting upon the arms, waiting for his daughter's return. When she came in and found him there, she started; it was the first time for the last six months that he had been home before her, and she knew that the Wesleyan service could not be over yet. What brought him there?

For some time the old man sat in silence, and his eyes followed her eagerly about the room; sharpened by anxiety, they noted what she was only just beginning to become conscious of herself. Suddenly he spoke, —

' Where have you been since church?'

' For a walk with Johnny Daly.'

He nodded. The directness of the answer pleased him.

' And what is there between you and Johnny Daly?' This time there was a sharper note of anxiety in his voice.

' We were afeard to tell you before, father, but I married him — three months ago — before the registrar.'

' Thank God!' said the old man solemnly. In his relief that it was no worse, and in his freshly awakened love for his daughter, he found it in his heart even to forgive his son-in-law for being a Catholic.

THE END.

Lightning Source UK Ltd.
Milton Keynes UK
UKHW02f1327060518
322147UK00022B/263/P